For more than forty years,
Yearling has been the leading name
in classic and award-winning literature
for young readers.

Yearling books feature children's
favorite authors and characters,
providing dynamic stories of adventure,
humor, history, mystery, and fantasy.

Trust Yearling paperbacks to entertain,
inspire, and promote the love of reading
in all children.

Also by N. D. Wilson

Leepike Ridge

Dandelion Fire

100 CUPBOARDS

⇥ BOOK I ⇤

N. D. WILSON

A YEARLING BOOK

Published by Yearling, an imprint of Random House Children's Books,
a division of Random House, Inc., New York

Visit us on the Web! www.randomhouse.com/kids
Educators and librarians, for a variety of teaching tools,
visit us at www.randomhouse.com/teachers
Visit www.100cupboards.com.

Library of Congress Cataloging-in-Publication Data
Wilson, N. D.   100 cupboards / N. D. Wilson.   p. cm.
Summary: After his parents are kidnapped, timid twelve-year-old Henry York
leaves his sheltered Boston life and moves to small-town Kansas, where he and his
cousin Henrietta discover and explore hidden doors in his attic room that seem to
open onto other worlds.
ISBN: 978-0-375-83881-1 (trade)—ISBN: 978-0-375-93881-8 (lib. bdg.)—
ISBN: 978-0-375-83882-8 (pbk.)
[1. Doors—Fiction. 2. Magic—Fiction. 3. Space and time—Fiction.
4. Cousins—Fiction. 5. Family life—Kansas—Fiction. 6. Kansas—Fiction.]
I. Title.   II. Title: One hundred cupboards.
PZ7.W69744Aac 2007   [Fic]—dc22   2007000164

Reprinted by arrangement with Random House Books for Young Readers

Printed in the United States of America
December 2008
20 19 18 17 16 15 14 13
First Yearling Edition

For my grandfathers:
Lt. Col. Lawrence Aubrey Greensides, USAF (Ret.),
and
Lt. James Irwin Wilson, USN (Ret.),
who tilled the soil of my imagination

1. Library/Adria/Lost
2. Cylinder/Aksum/Alt Pres
3. Wall/Mistra/CCM back
4. CV/Telmar/Alt Pas
5. Square/Ur/Damage
6. Barrow/Lindis/Pres
7. C. Lane/Yarnton/Vary delay?
8. /Endor/
9. Vestibule/Buda/Pre-war
10. Balcony/Fontevrault/apprx. C loss
11. Larder/Milan/Alt?
12. Lunar A./Carnassus/Alt Pas?
13. Spiral/Lahore/Ruin
14. Kustra/Damascus/III
15. Litter/Napata/Alt Pres
16. Stern/Tortuga/Static
17. Rail/Arizona/Now
18. Treb/Actium/Constant
19. Hutch/Fitzfaeren/Alt Pas?
20. Closet/Reba/Pres
21. Friez/Karatep/Broken
22. Deep Shaft/Masada/Varies
23. Viper/Edom/Alt
24. /Cleave/
25. Falls/Rauros/Alt
26. Drop/Ein Gedi/Alt 2M back?
27. Sealed/Daqin-Fulin/?
28. Bom J./Goa/Pres
29. Dome/Sintra/Alt pas
30. Hall/Cush/Damage
31. Partition/Globe, H-let/True pas? Alt?
32. Garden/H. Sophia/Pre-minaret alt
33. Wet/Henneth Annun/Alt
34. Encyc./Uqbar/Partial Pres
35. Lower Castile/Transito/Sealed pres?
36. Rotten/Heriot/?
37. Water Tunnel/Germa/Varies
38. Tempore/ /Alt pres?
39. Lake/Acacus/Now
40. Bowl/Skara Brae/Now
41. Lab/Knoss/Alt Pas. back 4M?
42. Inner p./Arcturus/Surging
43. Mound/Lerna/Now
44. Sewer/Topkapi/back 5C, true
45. Mouth/Marmara/Alt ?
46. ?/Angkor/Varies
47. Hall/Midge/Other
48. Fern/Bootes/Damage
49. /Cleave/
50. Peat/Grus/Trailing
51. Hole/Nara/Alt now
52. Konya/Huyuk/Shifting alt
53. Granary/Mohenjo/Lost
54. Pool/Basra/Slowing alt
55. Grave/Lagash/Damage
56. Commonwealth/Badon Hill/Same
57. Hostel?/Bovill/Now
58. Hollow/Iguazu/Shifting Now
59. Narbonne/Carcassone/back 3C
60. Daxiong/Ningbo/Now
61. Barn/Lower Sol/Alt pres
62. Gate/Procyon/Flux
63. Lighthouse/Alex/Alt Pres
64. Sheer/Henge/Never
65. Moss/Morte/Surging pres
66. ?/Kappa Crucis/Lost
67. Nave/Dochia/Alt Fut
68. Column/Thucyd/Alt
69. Corrund. shaft/Myanmar?/?
70. Pump/Rayfe/Fast
71. Vat/Kimber/Alt now
72. Southern Cit./Boghazk/Alt pas. back 3M
73. Bank/Amster/yesterday
74. Wells/Premier Cullinan/Lost
75. Yellow Pine/Tindrill/?
76. Temp/Mysore/Alt pas. back 4C
77. Post/Byzanthamum/When?
78. Shifting/San I.O./Shift spring
79. Gunnery/Brush/Static
80. Crush/Corvus/Dead
81. W.house/Cam?/Bubon
82. Mill/Gilroy/Alt trailing L
83. Reka/Skocjan/Back? Alt?
84. Bell/Delphi/Other
85. Base/Massis/Alt back 3C
86. Canal/Tenochtitlan/Alt pres
87. Bog/Malden/Damage
88. Blue/Cataldo/Alt fut
89. Loft/Strickne/Now
90. Sub Pill. 56/Persepolis/Alt pas. back M
91. Frame/Tana Kirkos/Partial Lost
92. ?/Ellora/Damage
93. Mine Spurr/Tordrillo/Now
94. Mid/Izamel/Flux Alt
95. Veranda/Millbank. Rhod./Alt pas
96. Model/Saqqara/Lost
97. Cliff/Achil/Now
98. Offs/Epidauros/Constat Aristo

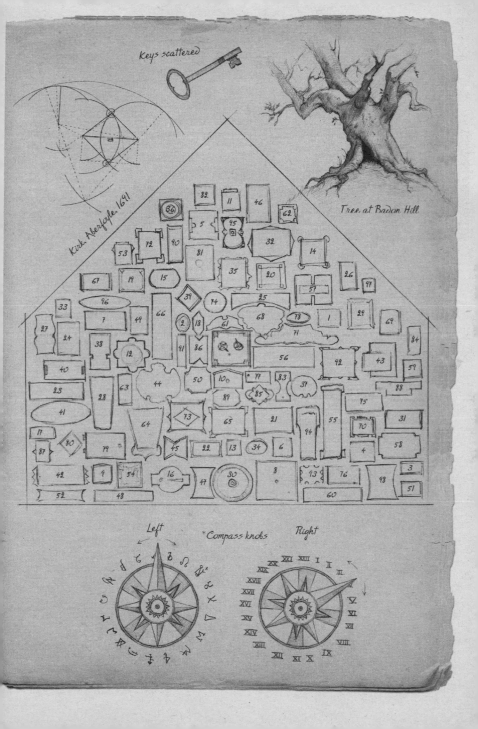

Keys scattered

Kirk, Aberfoyle 1691

Tree at Badon Hill

Left *Compass knobs Right

100 CUPBOARDS

CHAPTER ONE

Henry, Kansas, is a hot town. And a cold town. It is a town so still there are times when you can hear a fly trying to get through the window of the locked-up antique store on Main Street. Nobody remembers who owns the antique store, but if you press your face against the glass, like the fly, you'll see that whoever they are, they don't have much beyond a wide variety of wagon wheels. Yes, Henry is a still town. But there have been tornadoes on Main Street. If the wind blows, it's like it won't ever stop. Once it's stopped, there seems to be no hope of getting it started again.

There is a bus station in Henry, but it isn't on Main Street. It's one block north—the town fathers hadn't wanted all the additional traffic. The station lost one-third of its roof to a tornado fifteen years ago. In the same summer, a bottle rocket brought the gift of fire to its restrooms. The damage has never been repaired, but the town council makes sure that the building is painted fresh every other year, and always the color of a swimming pool. There is never graffiti. Vandals would have to drive more than twenty miles to buy the spray paint.

Every once in a long while, a bus creeps into town and eases to a stop beside the mostly roofed, bright aqua station with the charred bathrooms. Henry is always glad to see a bus. Such treats are rare.

On this day, the day our story begins, bus hopes were high. The Willis family was expecting their nephew, and the mister and missus stood on the curb waiting for his arrival.

Mrs. Willis couldn't hold nearly as still as the town. She was brimful of nervous energy and busily stepped on and off the curb as if she were waiting for the bus to take her off to another lifetime of grammar school and jump rope. She had planned to wear her best dress on principle—it was the sort of thing her mother would have done—but she had no idea which of her dresses was best, or how to begin the selection process. It was even possible that she didn't have a dress that was best.

So she had remained in her sweatpants and T-shirt. She had been canning in her kitchen and looked pleasant despite the faded teal of her pants. Her face was steam-ruddied and happy, and her brown hair, which had originally been pulled back into a ponytail, had struggled free. On this day, if you got close enough, as her nephew would when hugged, she smelled very strongly of peaches. She was of medium build in every direction, and she was called Dotty by her friends, Dots by her husband, and Mrs. Willis by everyone else.

People liked Dotty. They said she was interesting. They rarely did the same for her husband. They said Mr. Willis was thin, and they didn't just mean physically. They meant thin everywhere and every way. Dotty saw much more than thin, and she liked him. Frank Willis didn't seem to notice much of anything beyond that.

Mrs. Willis stopped her stepping and backed away from the curb. Something was shimmering on the highway. The bus was coming. She nudged Frank and pointed. He didn't seem to notice.

The Henry on the bus was not a town in Kansas. He was simply a twelve-year-old boy on a slow bus from Boston, waiting to meet an aunt and uncle he had not seen since the age of four. He was not looking forward to reuniting with Aunt Dotty and Uncle Frank. Not because he in any way disliked them, but because he had led a life that had taught him not to look forward to anything.

The bus stopped amid a shower of metallic grunts. Henry walked to the front, said goodbye to a talkative old woman, and stepped onto the curb into a lung-taste of diesel. The bus lurched off, the taste faded, and he found that he was being held tight by someone rather soft, though not large, and the smell of diesel had been replaced by peaches. His aunt held him back by the shoulders, her smile faded, and she became suddenly serious.

"We are both so sorry about your parents," she said. She was diligently eye-wrestling him. Henry couldn't quite look away. "But we are very happy you're going to be staying with us. Your cousins are all excited."

Someone patted Henry on the shoulder. He looked up.

"Yep," Uncle Frank said. He was watching the bus march out the other end of town. "The truck's over here," he added, and gestured with his head.

Uncle Frank carried Henry's duffel bag while Aunt Dotty escorted him to the truck, one arm tightly wrapped around his shoulder. It was an old truck. A few decades earlier, it may have been a Ford. Then it had been donated as a shop-class project to Henry High. Uncle Frank bought it at an end-of-the-year fundraiser. The paint was scum brown, the sort that normally hides at the bottom of a pond, attractive only to leeches and easily pleased frogs. The class had not been able to afford the bigger wheels they had dreamed of, so they had simply lifted the truck body as high as the instructor would allow. The overall effect was one of startling ricketiness. Henry's bag was thrown into the truck bed.

"Hop in," Uncle Frank said, and pointed in the back. "The tailgate doesn't drop, so just stand on the tire there and hoick yourself over. I'll boost you a bit."

Henry stood on the tire and teetered for a moment, trying to get one leg over the edge of the truck bed. Uncle Frank pushed him from behind, and he tumbled in onto his side.

Henry had never ridden in the back of a truck before, and he had always assumed it was illegal, though on the one trip his parents had taken him on, a tour of early Southwestern settlements, he had seen an entire truckload of field workers drive by. As he had been strapped into a car seat in the back of a Volvo at the time, he was extremely jealous. Only a few miles later, he had learned to his surprise that nine-year-old boys do not usually ride in car seats. A laughing school bus full of children taught him the lesson at a stoplight.

Henry perched himself on one of the truck's wheel wells and prepared for a spiritual experience. The engine fired its way into life, Frank forced reluctant metal gears together, and Henry slid off the wheel well into the truck bed as Henry, Kansas, swirled through his hair. They drove one block before the truck shifted its weight in the saddle and muscled around a right turn.

Henry slipped onto his back and spread-eagled so he wouldn't roll. Two blocks later, the truck bounced hard, and gravel rattled in the wheel wells like gunshots. Henry watched a rooster tail of dust climb into the sky behind the truck, and he tried to keep from banging his head every time the truck hopped a pothole. Eventually Uncle Frank stopped with a strong pull on the emergency brake, and Henry slid headfirst into the back of the cab. He picked himself carefully up onto all fours and peered at a pale blue house that he vaguely remembered. Aunt Dotty was grinning at him in the side mirror, pointing at the house and waving.

The house seemed big, and an even bigger barn hulked behind it. A mostly white cat sprawled in the yard, looking revolted by something or other. Old leaded-glass windows lined the first floor, a row of small windows the second, and one big, round window perched up in the eaves. On the front porch, below a long row of green-tarnished wind chimes, three girls stood staring at him.

Henry sat on the wood floor with his back to a wall. The three girls sat facing him, all cross-legged. They were in the attic. The whole room was open. The walls coved, and an old rail guarded the top of some very steep stairs. Henry was looking to his left, out the big, round window at the far end, trying to avoid staring at his cousins as much as they were staring at him. To Henry's right, at the other end of the attic, a pair of small doors led into a space that was no longer the attic closet and was now Henry's bedroom. Uncle Frank had apologized for the size and pointed out, before Aunt Dotty threw an elbow to his ribs, that if Henry's parents were never heard from again and Henry had to live with them always, they would go ahead and knock the wall down and expand his room a bit.

Henry had thanked him.

"I'm Anastasia," the smallest girl said.

"I know," said Henry. She was the youngest, small and wiry for a nine-year-old. And freckled. Her hair was brown, but Henry thought it looked like it wanted to be red.

"Then how come you didn't say 'Hello, Anastasia' right off? Were you just being rude?"

"Hush," the oldest girl said.

Anastasia wrinkled her lip. "If you knew I was Anastasia, then what are their names?"

Henry looked to the oldest girl. Her straight, nearly black hair hung loose past her shoulders. She smiled at him.

"Penny," Henry said. He turned to the third girl, who had thick brown curls and green eyes. "And Henrietta."

Henrietta was staring at him. Henry looked away. He suspected he had done something rather awful to Henrietta's cat on his last visit. Suddenly the memory appeared vividly in the foreground of his mind and danced an emphatic jig. He turned red and Anastasia started talking again.

"What's Penny *stand* for?" she asked, narrowing her eyes.

Penny smiled and pulled her crossed legs tighter. "It doesn't stand for anything, Anastasia."

"It stands for Penelope," Anastasia insisted. "Doesn't it, Henry?" Henry shrugged, but Anastasia wasn't looking at him. She was looking at Henrietta.

Henrietta ignored her.

"No," Penny said. "It's *short* for Penelope, it doesn't *stand* for it. Standing for something is when you just do initials."

Henry tried to catch Henrietta's eye. "Do they call you Henry?" he asked.

"Yes," Henrietta said. Henry watched her jaw clench. "I don't like it," she added.

"Henrietta's too long," Anastasia said.

Henry thought for a moment. "It's no longer than Anastasia." He double-checked the syllables in his head. "Yeah."

"For a while I wanted to be called Josephine, but

then they just called me Jo." Henrietta looked at Henry. "Will you call me Beatrice?"

"Um, sure," Henry said.

"We'll call you Beat," Anastasia said, smiling.

"No, you won't," Henrietta said. "Not if you want to keep your teeth."

"Stop it," Penny said. "Why don't we just call you Henrietta? Now that *he's* here, we can't call you Henry."

Henrietta considered this option. She looked at Henry. She seemed to want him to agree.

"Okay," Henry said. They were silent again, and Henry's thoughts wandered back through his tour of the house.

The revolted cat—one of the girls had called him Blake—had quickly disappeared while Aunt Dotty led Henry onto the porch and very helpfully said, "Henry, you remember the girls."

Henry had then been attached to a human train, one back from the engine, on a high-speed tour of the house. He had seen sofas, gifts from dead great-aunts, lamps that didn't work, treasures acquired by Uncle Frank on the Internet (including a fish fossil now being used, uniquely and quite cheaply, Dotty pointed out, as an end table). Fingers pointed down the stairs into a dark basement. Various artistic pieces were highlighted, all produced by Frank and the girls. Aunt

Dotty had laughed and called them "especially local artists." Henry was shown the junk drawer, containing a small flashlight, a box of rubber bands, and a sedimentary layer of pens, pencils, paper clips, glue, and a plastic box with a picture of the ocean on its lid. He had seen the toilet, been shown the plunger, and heard of the plumbing trouble. He had been told to hold still and listen to see if the fridge would make its funny noise. It hadn't, but he had been warned that he would know when it did. And on the big second-story landing, there had been the door to the room at the front of the house. Henrietta had called it Grandfather's room, but no one had gone near it. Every other door in the house, every cabinet, every drawer, and every cupboard, had all been opened. But not that one.

Henry's mind snapped back. He was still on the floor in the attic. The girls had not yet grown weary of him and departed.

"Henry?" Anastasia said. "Henry, do you think your parents are going to die?"

Penny shot an eye-rebuke in her sister's direction, but it went unheeded. Henrietta and Anastasia were staring at Henry. Henrietta began twisting her hair.

Anastasia leaned forward. "Zeke Johnson's dad got killed by a combine."

"Stop it!" Penelope said. "If you don't want to talk about it, Henry . . ."

"Penelope likes Zeke," Anastasia said. Henrietta laughed.

Penelope darkened. "Everyone likes Zeke," she said.

Anastasia looked right into Henry's eyes. "He goes up to the graveyard by himself," she said. "And he pitches baseballs at his dad's gravestone."

Penelope crossed her arms. "Mr. Simon told him to write his dad a goodbye letter and he didn't want to. So he pitched to him instead."

"I don't want to talk about Zeke," Henrietta said. "Penny always talks about Zeke. I want to hear about Uncle Phil and Aunt Ursula."

"Do you think they're going to die?" Anastasia asked again.

Penelope sniffed. "You don't have to, Henry."

Henry pulled in a deep breath and then sighed. "No, it's okay. I don't know much, anyway. They got taken hostage riding their bicycles in Colombia. The men who talked to me at school said they would be ransomed back."

"What were they doing?" Henrietta asked.

"They're travel writers, and they wanted to write a book about bicycling across South America. They've been doing stuff like that ever since I was old enough to go to school."

"You've been to a lot of places, then," Henrietta said.

"No," Henry said. "They never take me with them. I've been to Disney World, but that was with a nanny. And California once."

Anastasia leaned forward. "Your parents really got kidnapped?" she asked. Henry nodded. "By guys with guns? Do you think they had masks? Your parents might be tied up in a cave somewhere right now."

"I don't know. Something like that," Henry said. "They got kidnapped, anyway."

The three girls were impressed, and they sat, chewing on lips or nails, examining Henry and quietly contemplating the situation.

After a moment, Frank's voice climbed loudly up the stairs. "Scrub the bones!" he yelled, and the attic echoed.

"What?" Henry asked.

The girls picked themselves up off the floor.

"Teeth," Henrietta said. "Brush your teeth."

CHAPTER TWO

Henry was having trouble falling asleep. Aunt Dotty had made up his bed while he was brushing his teeth, and Uncle Frank had shoved a swamp cooler from the basement into the round window at the end of the attic. Henry had never seen a swamp cooler before, but he assumed it was pretty much the same as the air conditioners that stuck out of the wall under hotel windows. Only this one was leaning a little dangerously to one side and was packed in place with old overalls.

Henry's room contained his bed, on which he sprawled, a little stand that looked like it was meant to hold a fake fern but now held a reading lamp, and a three-drawer dresser. His doors were open. Henry wanted the full benefit of the swamp cooler.

Henry's light was off. There was no reason to have it on. The only thing to look at in his little room was a poster on the ceiling, and he'd finished staring at it a long time ago. Uncle Frank said that it had been his when he was young. It was a picture of the University of Kansas basketball team. One of them, at least. And not a very good one, Henry thought. None of the guys looked athletic.

Because of the moon, the attic was almost brighter without Henry's lamp. It hung low in the sky and its light climbed in the window, sloshing silently around the floor and silvering the walls. Henry watched the silver light until his eyes began to water. He wasn't blinking. He was too awake to blink. He wondered if there was any chance that this summer he would get to play baseball. He would have to learn to throw first. And he'd have to make sure that no one saw him learning.

Henry hoped his parents would be all right. He even hoped they would come back. But he also thought it would be nice if they came back at the end of the summer, right before he went back to school, or whenever the baseball season ended.

Henry was thinking about baseball and his uncle's truck, as well as what exactly it was his aunt had smelled like when she hugged him, when something thumped against the wall above his head. He landed gently on his bed before he even realized that he'd jumped in surprise. He forced himself to breathe, still not blinking.

"Some bird," he said loudly. He was not going to whisper. "Probably an owl or a bat or something."

Henry tried to force his eyes shut, not noticing when they popped back open. Whatever had thumped outside of his wall was now scratching. Or he was imagining that it was. He couldn't be sure. Yes, he could. It thumped again, not as loudly, but still a genuine thump.

Henry sat up in bed and tried to breathe normally, picturing large bats scrambling on the house and rats trekking through the walls. No different from thousands of noises in thousands of nights, he told himself. Roll over. Ignore it. Instead, he got out of bed and walked to the stairs. He would go to the bathroom. He would run water and flush a toilet. He would wash his mind with normal noise.

Leaving behind the moonlit attic was like stepping into a hole, and the steep stairs squealed at him as he went.

Someone had left the light on in the bathroom— a band of glow at the bottom of the door frosted the carpeted landing. When he reached the door, Henry put his hand out for the knob and froze. Someone was probably inside. No one would leave the light on and then shut the door.

Henry hated knocking. He hated conversations through bathroom doors. So he dropped his hand and turned to go sit on the stairs and wait. He hadn't taken a step when the knob turned. Henry caught his breath, jumped toward the stairs, and sat down in the darkness.

An old man stepped onto the landing. He was short and had a polished bald head with white hair straggling off the sides. Long tweed trousers were rolled up at his ankles, and a purple satin bathrobe hung down around a dirty white T-shirt. The bottom of the bathrobe piled on the floor around the man's bare feet.

The man was daubing shaving cream off his neck with a hand towel. He sniffed loudly and brought the towel up to his face while he turned toward Grandfather's bedroom door at the end of the landing. The purple robe dragged behind him like the train on a wedding dress. Before he touched the door, he looked back over his shoulder. His deep black eyes settled on Henry in the darkness.

Henry blinked hard and then yawned, stretching his arms above his head. Someone had left the bathroom light on, but the door was open. Why was he sitting on the stairs? He wasn't sure, but he needed to use the bathroom.

He did, and then hurried back up the stairs into his attic.

Henry slid into his bed with his mind wandering aimlessly, looking for something it had lost. He knew he had forgotten something, but he didn't notice when one blink was too heavy to reopen. He was somewhere else, dreaming of a field where he knew how to throw a ball. And for some reason, a man in a purple robe was watching.

CHAPTER THREE

Henry slept for a long time. He woke because he couldn't sleep any longer. His body was full. He picked himself up out of bed, pulled on his jeans and a T-shirt, and felt his way down the steep stairs with feet a little soft from sleep. He found his aunt in the kitchen.

"Henry!" she said, and grinned at him. She was still canning. Her hair was staggering away from her temples, and her face was tomato red above a faded green apron. An enormous black pot boiled on the stove. "We were about to send out a search-and-rescue team." She laughed and cranked a contraption that was pulping wrinkly apples. Henry stared at the long snake of peels and cores and nastiness that was crawling out of one end. Dotty looked back at him and laughed again. "Don't you look down on my apples, Henry York! The worms add to the flavor. Cold cereal's on the shelf behind you if you like, and I'd think you would after coming out of hibernation. Bowl's on the counter. Milk's in the fridge."

18

"Thanks," Henry said, and began assembling his breakfast. He was used to milk with transparent edges, milk that looked a little blue. This milk looked more like cream. It was thick, white, and coated the cereal with film as Henry poured. In his mouth, he could feel it clinging to his tongue. His tongue didn't mind.

Dotty dumped a bowl of pulped cores into the trash and turned around.

"Well, then, Henry York," she said. "When you're finished there, you can rinse out your bowl. Then, unless you want to go back to bed and sleep through another meal, you can head out to the barn. Your uncle wants to talk with you. You should have it to yourselves. The girls are off in town for a birthday." She wiped her hands on her apron and turned back to her work.

Henry, licking his teeth, walked out of the kitchen, through mounds of boots in the mudroom, and onto the back porch. The overgrown lawn drifted downhill to the foot of the barn. Beyond the barn, flat fields stretched to the horizon, broken only by irrigation ditches and the occasional dirt road. The rest was all sky.

Henry stood and stared blankly at the landscape. At another time, it would have affected him. He would have marveled at the flatness, at the bareness, at how much space could fit into a single view. Instead, he wandered through his sleep-cobwebbed mind, trying to sort and straighten thoughts just as filmy as his teeth and tongue.

Distracted, Henry walked down to the barn. The door was a puzzle. It was a slider, and he couldn't get the metal lever to unlatch. When he did finally succeed in jerking it up, he couldn't persuade the big plank door to plow along its rusty runners. With a slip and a stagger, he got it in the end and walked inside, too curious about the contents of the barn to notice his rust-stained hands. It was bigger inside than he had expected. There were old plank stalls along both sides. A Weed Eater and three bicycles dangled from the beams.

"Henry? That you down there?" Uncle Frank's voice fell through the ceiling above him. "Come on up. There's a ladder at the end."

Henry found the ladder, nailed to the wall and completely vertical. He stepped onto the lowest rung, a dry, dirty board, and stared up the ladder shaft—up past two levels, up to the underside of the barn's beamed ceiling. There had been a ladder on Henry's bunk bed, and that was as high as he'd ever climbed.

"Henry?" his uncle yelled.

"Yeah, I'm coming, Uncle Frank."

"All the way up. I'm in the loft."

Henry started climbing. If he fell, there would be an enormous dust cloud where he landed. Would Uncle Frank even hear him? How long would he lie there? What would he look like to Frank, from up in the loft? He shivered.

As he climbed through the second level, he glanced around. Large pink chalk clouds decorated the floor beside a hopscotch grid. He quickly scrambled up the last couple of rungs and stuck his head through the floor into the loft.

"Heya, Henry," Uncle Frank said. He was sitting at a desk buried in stuff. "You like the climb?"

"Sure," Henry said, breathing hard. He came the rest of the way up and stepped off the ladder.

Frank smiled. "It goes higher. Up all the way to the roost. Climb on up if you like. There's a little door you can throw open, and a shelf that's pretty much pigeon world. You have to be careful. It gets slick if they've been there recently. It's probably the highest elevation in Kansas, not counting other barns and the silos. There's some big ones around here."

"Silos?" Henry asked, looking toward the roost. "Like where they store grain?"

"That's what I mean," Frank said. "Now, Henry, I want to tell you something. Your aunt doesn't know about it, and I might not even tell her for a good while.

But I need to spill beans to somebody, and here you are."

"What is it?" Henry pulled his eyes down from the roost and looked at his uncle. Frank had a computer on an old buffet, a hutch full of doors and drawers. The monitor sat in the middle, surrounded by mounds of knickknacks—jumbled figurines, small vases, and tools. Henry could see a hatchet handle and a miniature Canadian flag in one pile, half a model ship in another.

Frank leaned back in his chair and curled his lips against his teeth. "I got a store on the Internet, and I sell things to people all over the world. Been doing it for almost two months now, and today I've struck it rich!" Frank laughed. "I've just sold two tumbleweeds for fifteen hundred dollars."

"Who'd buy tumbleweed?" Henry asked. "That's a lot of money."

Frank grinned and put his hands behind his head. "Yes, it is. I would have been happy with ten dollars for the both of them, but some Japanese businessmen got their blood up for the weeds, fought it out with each other, and here I sit, a wealthy man. That's seven hundred and fifty dollars a pop."

"Wow," Henry said. "Do you really think they'll pay?"

"Sure they will." He straightened and slid forward

in his chair. "Are you busy with something? How about we ride into town for some ice cream and then go pickin' money? Run in and tell your aunt we're going. I'll be in just after I e-mail my new client."

Henry didn't ride in the back of the truck this time. He bounced and jostled between the door and the long prong of the stick shift. He was not buckled. He had waited to be told, but now he suspected that wouldn't happen.

Henry cranked his window down, put his arm out, and leaned his face into the wind. They were going all the way to the other side of town, his uncle had said, and so they had taken the farm roads around rather than driving straight through. Henry's father had given him a book on city planning for Christmas, so he couldn't help thinking of the road as a sort of beltway, a ring road. Only it's gravel, Henry thought. And barely two lanes.

He stopped thinking about cities and watched the town of Henry slide past to his right. He was thrown against his door and bounced up to the roof as the truck failed to leap a pothole. The window handle dug into his leg, and he hit his head on something. Still, he didn't buckle. He did, however, sneak his hand up when he thought his uncle wasn't looking and lock his door.

Locusts were flying up in front of the truck and spinning off in its wake when Frank turned right to connect to the main road and reenter the town from the other side.

"Is that really faster?" Henry asked.

"Nope," Frank said. "Just more fun. No point in taking a truck like this down Main Street except when we're heading to the barbershop or closer."

The two of them began with ice cream at a gas station. Then they pressed their faces on the window of the closed antique shop, squinting at stacks of wheels in the dusty darkness. The ice cream made Frank hungry, so he took Henry to a place called Lenny's, owned by a man named Kyle, and they ate flat cheeseburgers and thick fries. In a town smaller than Henry had first imagined, they managed to dawdle away the afternoon, going from place to place for one reason or another or no reason at all. Until finally they arrived at the city park and a rummage sale run by senior citizens beneath a sagging pavilion.

As Henry climbed out of the truck, an old woman in a red vest told him to make sure to spend his money, because all of it would go toward the Fourth of July fireworks at the football field.

Henry didn't have any money, and he wasn't all

that interested in the rummage sale. He sat down with his back to a pole.

"Hey, Henry!" Frank yelled across three rows of tables. "You got a glove?"

"A glove?" Henry blinked. "What do you mean?"

"Baseball glove," Frank said. "You got one? 'Ope, never mind, it's a lefty."

Henry sat up. "I'm left-handed," he said. "But I don't think I want it. I don't really like baseball." Which is what many people say when they mean "I'm not any good."

"Well, get on over here and try it on. Boy needs a glove."

Henry didn't need to try it on. If he had a glove, then someone would want to play catch, and he would have to throw. He wanted to practice before that happened. Still, he stood up and picked his way through the rows of tables until he stood in front of his uncle. The leather was dark and old. Hairline cracks stood out on the thick fingers, but the palm was shiny smooth. Henry slid his hand inside. It fit nicely.

"We'll oil it up when we get home." Frank took Henry's gloved hand and held it up to his face. "Smell that leather," he said. "Specially treated with dirt, sweat, and ten thousand catches. An old glove's the best glove. You can't buy history new."

* * *

When they left the rummage sale, Frank stowed a wide-bodied lamp and an incomplete set of encyclopedias in the back of the truck. And Henry was not only the fearful owner of a new baseball glove, but also a knife. It was a lock-blade that didn't lock, and it felt strange in his hand. His parents had never prohibited his owning a knife, probably because it had never crossed their minds that he might get one. Henry held the blade open and touched its edge with his finger.

"Pretty dull now," Frank said, taking his eyes off the dirt road. "But I'll sharpen it up for you. Dotty's got the sharpest knives I know of. Can't tolerate a dull knife. Anybody half smart keeps their knives sharp."

"Does she ever cut herself?"

"I'll tell you a little secret, Henry, a secret that everybody knows. It's the dull knife that cuts you." Frank leaned over and slapped Henry's knee. "You aren't gonna slip whittling with a sharp blade. And if you did, the cut would be cleaner and easier to tend. Sharp knives are safer. Fact. I'd even recommend you not go carving anything until I get out my kit and put an edge on that blade."

"Okay, Uncle Frank." Henry let go of the blade, and it dropped limply back into the handle. "How come it won't stay open?"

Frank drummed his fingers on the wheel. "Oh,

somethin' or other's busted on the inside. I've had lots of knives like that. Doesn't make much difference unless it comes open in your pocket. I've still got a scar from when one did that. Forgot I had it with me and slid into second base. Just press your thumb down on the side of the blade when you've got it open and you'll be fine. Gets you a much stronger grip, too."

"Okay," Henry said. He didn't put the knife back in his pocket.

Uncle Frank pulled the truck onto a dirt patch that straddled a ditch and faded into the field.

"Here we are, Henry. Tumbleweeds are like people. They tend to collect someplace out of the wind."

"What?" Henry asked. Frank was already getting out of the truck.

"It's not just people and weeds," Frank said. "It's everything." He stepped down into the ditch. A trickle of water ran along the bottom and into a culvert. Tangled and muddy, tumbleweed clung to the culvert mouth and rustled around Frank's legs as he moved. He grabbed the matted weeds, lifted them up, and threw a pile onto the gravel shoulder. The bottom of the lump dripped brown water.

"You ever wonder, Henry, how bits of dust find each other on the floor?" Frank began kicking the remaining weeds into a mound. "Some part of a blade of grass gets eaten by a cow and dropped out its back end, where it dries in the sun and gets trampled. Then some wind picks it up, and, of all the little bits of nothing much in the world, it comes in your window and lands on your floor."

Henry watched while Frank scrambled out of the ditch and threw the tumble-blobs into the back of the truck.

"Then," Frank continued, brushing off his hands, "that little bit of dust meets another little bit of dust, only it came off your sweater, which was cut from some sheep in New Zealand, and the two bits grab some of your hair and some other hair that you picked up on your shirt from a booth in a restaurant, and then they get kicked around until they all roll under your bed and hide in the corner."

Frank was trying to tie down the weeds with string.

"It's the same with people. If they're a little lost, they get blown around until they drop into some shelter or hole or culvert."

He snapped off the end of the twine and climbed back into the truck. Henry climbed back in beside him.

"There are holes like that in cities," he said, "in houses—anyplace. Holes where the lost things stop."

"Like where?" Henry asked.

Frank laughed and started the truck. "Like belly buttons. Like here. And Cleveland. Henry is on a much smaller scale, so fewer people drift here. And when they climb out, they end up pushed around until they come to rest someplace else."

Henry watched Uncle Frank shift into gear.

"I was lost once," Frank said, and looked over at him. "But I'm found now. I'm under the bed. I'm in the same culvert you are. Only, I don't think you're done tumblin'."

Despite the string Frank had thrown across the truck bed, pairs and clusters of tumbleweed gusted away every few hundred yards as they drove home.

"That's how rich I am," Frank said when Henry pointed out one particularly large cluster in the road behind them. "Thousands of dollars flyin' out of my truck and I'm not even gonna slow down. If I was half smart, I would have brought a tarp. Let's see if I can lose all of them before our turn."

He punched the gas. A column of dust, flying gravel, and the occasional bouncing weed followed them all the way home.

When they arrived, Frank pulled the truck into the grass and drove across the lawn, around the house, and straight up to the barn. Henry kicked his door open and walked back to where Frank stood beside the tailgate. There were four weeds tangled up in the string, hanging behind the truck. Frank's rummage-sale lamp had lost its shade, and the box of encyclopedias had tipped over and spilled its contents against the tailgate.

"Hmm," Uncle Frank said. Henry didn't say anything. "Sometimes, Henry, I do wish I had a bit more of your aunt Dotty in me. Grab those weeds and throw 'em in one of the horse stalls. I'm gonna get a tarp and run back out real quick. You stay here. Don't tell your aunt what we've been doin'."

"Okay," Henry said.

After dinner, Dotty and Frank went out to the front porch for the one smoke Frank was allowed per day. Henry followed the girls to their room and collapsed onto the floor. He had accepted Uncle Frank's offer to divvy up the girls' leftover meat loaf, and now there was more meat inside him than there had ever been in the history of his life. Probably more ketchup, too. His cousins were talking around him, but he couldn't make his mind listen.

A population of dolls was scattered throughout the room. Some, china-skinned and delicate, stood in a line across the top of the dresser, each propped up by its own metal stand. A few others, with floppy limbs and stitched features, sprawled on beds, and one, a plastic child, lay on its side looking at Henry. One of its eyes was shut.

A little creepy, Henry thought. But then, he'd never been around a doll that hadn't been used in primitive rituals. His parents had been bringing those back from their trips for as long as he could remember.

A bunk bed filled one side of the room, a smaller bed squatted on the other, and a big window between them looked out on the barn. The view from Henry's room would have been nearly identical if he'd had a window.

"Why do all three of you share a room?" he asked, trying to sit up. He lay back down quickly. "This is a really big house." He was interrupting a disagreement over whether everyone should play pirates or Monopoly. The advocate of the board game was Henrietta; of pirates, Anastasia. Penelope lay on the top bunk, unaffected, fully aware that she was the swing vote but ignoring the whole discussion. She was reading something.

"It is," Penelope said, putting down her book. "There is another room on the first floor, but it's Mom's sewing room. And it's where Dad keeps the television. I wonder if he would let us watch it tonight?"

"There are three bedrooms on this floor," Anastasia said. She was sitting on the top bunk by Penny's feet. "Mom and Dad's, this one, and . . ."

"Grandfather's," Henrietta finished. She looked in Henry's eyes. "He's dead."

"Really?" Henry asked. "I thought—" He stopped suddenly. He'd known his grandfather had died. He remembered his mother calling him at school. But he was remembering something else, too. Except that he couldn't. Not quite. He could only remember that he was forgetting something. His cousins were looking at him. He blinked.

"Yeah," he said. His face felt hot. "I knew that."

"Grandfather's is the best," Penelope continued. Anastasia and Henrietta both tried to cut in, but Penelope just spoke louder. "It's got a huge bed, because he was so tall, and the two windows right on the front of the house. Mom and Dad will take it once they get it unlocked. Dad lost the key. He thinks it's on his desk somewhere."

"And he won't call the locksmith even though Mom wants him to," Henrietta added. "Says he's a sneak, and he'll fix it himself."

"The windows won't open, either," Penelope said.

"And there's the attic," Anastasia said. "Where you live. You get the whole thing. Mom says we can't play up there anymore unless we ask."

"Shhh," Penelope said.

"Who locked Grandfather's room?" Henry asked.

"Mom thinks it isn't locked, just broken," Penelope said. The other girls nodded. "Dad says old doors do funny things."

"How long has it been broken?"

"Since Grandfather died," Penelope said. "Two years ago."

"It's been locked for two years?" Henry asked.

Penelope nodded.

"And no one has been in there since?" Henry climbed to his feet. He opened the girls' door and stepped onto the landing. "That's the one, right?" He was whispering.

"Yeah," Henrietta said.

Henry walked slowly down the landing, past Frank and Dotty's room, and past the bathroom. The girls, all silent, watched him. The door to Grandfather's room looked old but normal enough. The stained brass handle drooped. Henry put out his hand, then stopped. His eyes weren't focused on what was in front of him. They were straining at an image in his head. A short old man. Was he purple? Dressed in purple? In a purple dress? A short old man in a purple robe was watching him play baseball.

"See? Watch." Henry jumped at Henrietta's voice in his ear. She jiggled the handle. "Now c'mon. Let's go do something."

"I don't want to play Monopoly or pirates," Anastasia said.

"Fine," Penelope said. "Hopscotch Cannibals. I'll even play with you kids for a bit." She looked at Henry. "They do it in the barn."

"Like you're so old," Anastasia said. She turned to Henry. "She *invented* Hopscotch Cannibals."

Penelope started down the stairs. "When I was little," she said.

"Were you little last summer?" Henrietta asked.

The three girls disappeared as they descended. For a moment, Henry stood looking at Grandfather's door.

"Henry?" Anastasia yelled. And Henry followed them.

Henry tried to play. And while he enjoyed being up in the barn and jumping around and watching the dust fly, the game was a little embarrassing. He was not above make-believe, he just usually did it by himself in his room.

So Henry left the girls, descended the ladder, and wandered over to the house and inside. He borrowed a tattered old book from Uncle Frank titled *Up Periscope* and climbed the flights of stairs to his room in the attic, glancing at Grandfather's room as he went. The sun was not long down, and he sat on his bed looking out his doors, across the length of the attic, and out the round window at a few of the flickering, halfhearted, or malfunctioning streetlights in Henry, Kansas. After a while, he shut his doors, leaned back on his bed wondering what sort of book Frank had given him, and fell asleep with his light on.

*   *   *

Henry jerked awake and squinted in the light. At first, he wasn't sure why he was awake. He didn't need to use the bathroom, his arms weren't asleep, and he wasn't hungry. He couldn't have been sleeping long.

He sat up. A piece of plaster rolled down his forehead, bounced on the tip of his nose, and landed on his chest. He ran one hand through his hair, and more bits of his wall dropped onto his lap. He looked up.

Above him, two small knobs protruded from the plaster of his wall. One of the knobs was turning, very slightly. A small scraping noise grew until a final thump rained fine plaster dust down on Henry and his bed.

For a few minutes, Henry simply stared—holding his breath, breathing heavily, and then holding it again. The knobs were so perfectly still that he began to wonder if one had actually moved. He had been sleeping. He could have dreamed it.

I didn't dream it, he told himself. They're right there, sticking through my wall. Henry knew what was on the other side of the wall—absolutely nothing. One floor down, the girls' window looked out over the fields, and beneath that, there was the kitchen wall, a mudroom door, and the grass that ran down to the barn.

Henry turned around and carefully poked at the

knobs, then began picking chunks of plaster off the wall. Leaving a pile of dust on his blanket, he cleared out the area around both knobs and discovered a square metal door no more than eight inches wide, tarnished and stained green and brown under the dust. He leaned forward to take a closer look at the knobs themselves. His shadow wouldn't get out of the way, so he brought his lamp over onto the bed beside him.

The knobs were in the center of the door. They were a very old and dull brass, slender—hardly knobs at all—with filthy broad skirts. Henry took one in each hand and turned them. They spun easily and silently, but nothing happened. One large arrow stuck out of each skirt. Around the left-hand knob, symbols had been inlaid into the door, and around the knob on the right, numerals. The symbols on the left began with *A* and ended—back beside the *A*—with something like a *G*. He didn't recognize the others. The knob on the right was simpler. It was surrounded by letters that he knew were actually numbers: I to XXII in Roman numerals. He counted the strange alphabet on the left and found that there were nineteen letters.

Henry had never been terribly good at math, but he knew he would have to multiply nineteen by twenty-two to find out how many possible combinations there could be to open the door. But knowing what he needed to do and being able to do it were two different things. After several attempts to do the math in his head, he left his room and went as quietly as he could down his stairs, to the second-story landing, and down again. He was less careful once he was on the first floor and made his way quickly into the kitchen, where he began rooting through the junk drawer for a pencil. He found a pen and a small instruction manual for a blender. He tore the back page off and hurried upstairs.

Back in the attic, Henry ran on his toes straight to his small room and knelt on his bed. The knobs had not disappeared. He scratched out the math on his bit of paper: 22 times 19 was . . . 418. Henry sat back and looked at the number: 418 was a lot.

"What are you doing?" a voice asked from behind him. Henrietta stood in his doorway. Her thick hair stuck out from her head and a pillow crease ran down her cheek, but her eyes were bright. "I heard you coming down the stairs." She stepped into his room, looking past him. "What did you do to the wall?"

Henry coughed and unswallowed his Adam's apple. "I didn't do anything. It just cracked, and I was trying to see what was underneath the plaster." Henry turned to the wall. "I found this little door. And it won't open unless you know the combination, and I figured out that there are 418 possible combinations and only one of them will work, and I'm going to try all of them until I get it open."

Henrietta knelt on the bed beside him. "What do you think's inside?" she asked.

Henry sat quietly for a moment. "I don't know yet," he admitted.

"Yes, but what do you think?"

Henry searched his mind for anything that could be kept behind small, hidden doors.

"Somebody's old things, maybe," he said. "Socks or a pair of shoes. Some old fountain pens would be cool."

"Oh," Henrietta said. "I was thinking there might be a map or a book explaining how to get to a secret city. Keys to a forgotten door or something. Maybe diamonds."

"Well," Henry said, "I think I should start trying to get it open. I'm going to start backward. I'll put this arrow on the last letter and then try it with all of the Roman numerals. Then I'll do the next letter with all the Roman numerals, until I've done all 418."

"Okay," said Henrietta, and she plopped back onto the bed to watch as Henry began turning the knobs and pulling on them. "I hope it's a map," she added.

Henry had finished three and a half letters before she interrupted him for the first time.

"How many are left, Henry?"

Henry stopped and thought. "I've done 76. I can't subtract 76 from 418 in my head, but there are more than 300 left."

He was done with five letters when she interrupted again.

"Henry, what are those other marks on the knobs?"

"What marks?" he asked.

"Those ones," Henrietta said, and she sat up on her knees and licked her thumbs. Henry moved out of her way and watched her rub the knobs clean. The large arrows he had been using stuck out of the knobs. When Henrietta sat back down, Henry could see three more arrows on each knob. Much smaller and on the surface of the skirts only, they divided the knobs into quarters.

"They look like compasses," Henrietta said. "See? The big arrow is how they do north on maps, and then there's south, east, and west. I bet there is a map in there. What else would be behind compass knobs?"

Henry didn't answer. He slumped.

"What's wrong?" Henrietta asked.

Henry flopped all the way back on the bed and clicked his teeth. "We'll never get it open."

"We won't? Why not?" she asked. "Stop grinding your teeth. There can't be that many left."

"There's way more. I don't even know how to find

out how many more. With four pointers on each knob, there could be thousands of combinations."

"Oh," she said. "Maybe we should go to bed. We can figure it out tomorrow."

"Yeah. We should go to bed." He looked at his blanket. "But first I should clean this up."

Henrietta stood and stretched. "Just take it downstairs and shake it outside."

Henry pulled his blanket up by its four corners and slung it over his shoulder like a sack. Then the two of them left his room and crept carefully down the stairs. They reached the girls' room, whispered good night, and Henrietta hurried to her bunk. Henry continued downstairs to the mudroom. Stepping outside, he decided to go a little ways from the house so nobody would see plaster on the lawn. His bare feet were swallowed by the cool grass, but he didn't notice. He was staring up at an enormous sky, heavily dusted with stars. A glaring two-thirds of a moon sat just above the horizon. He made his way down to the barn, went around the side, shook out his blanket, and sat down.

Henry had never heard of such a thing as a forgotten door. Back at school, he never would have believed such things existed. But here was different. There was something strange about here. He felt just like he had when he'd found out that kids his age don't ride in car seats and that boys pee standing up. He remembered unpacking his bags at boarding school while his roommate watched. His roommate had asked him what the helmet was for, and Henry had suddenly had the suspicious sensation that he had been kept in the dark, that the world was off behaving in one way while he, Henry, wore a helmet. He had barely prevented himself from answering his roommate honestly. The words "It's a helmet my mom bought me to wear in PE" were replaced with "It's for racing. I don't think I'll need it here."

Whatever was going on inside the wall in his room was much bigger than finding out that other boys didn't have to wear helmets. If there really were forgotten doors and secret cities, and maps and books to tell you how to find them, then he needed to know. He looked around at the tall, dew-chilly grass and for a moment didn't see grass. Instead, he saw millions of slender green blades made of sunlight and air, thick on the ground and gently blowing, tickling his now-damp feet, and all the while silently pulling life up out of the earth. Each was another kid without a helmet, a kid who knew how things were actually done.

Above him, the stars twinkled with laughter. Galaxies looked. Nudged each other. Chuckled.

"He didn't know about secret cities," Orion said. "His mother never told him."

The Great Bear smiled. "Did his dad tell him about forgotten doors?"

"Never."

"Journals?"

"Only having to do with science projects or bicycle trips."

"Maps?"

"Mostly topographic, or the kind that shade countries in different colors based on gross national product or primary exports."

"Nothing with 'Here be dragons' on the edges?"

"Never. He found a hidden cupboard with compass locks, and do you know what he thought was in it?"

"A unicorn's horn?"

"Socks."

"Socks?"

"Or pens."

"Pens?"

Henry sighed. "I don't even know how to work compass locks," he said. He stood and started back to the house with a familiar feeling, the feeling of *Now I know*. The feeling that means tonight you will sneak down to the dormitory Dumpster with your helmet, a stack of nightgowns, and your therapeutic bear. The feeling of *Tomorrow I will have changed*.

Henry walked into the kitchen and saw his knife on the counter. He picked it up and flipped it open. The

...dge smiled at him. Pinning it open

The wind scratched its ...ed through the house to his

The stars swung slowly across the ... of the barn.
and the grass swayed and grew, content to world,
world's carpet but still desiring to be taller.

Henry knelt on his bed upstairs and pried plaster
off the wall with his knife. His thumb ached.

When day came to Kansas, its light crept in the round attic window and slid over the swamp cooler, stretching out across the old floor and some of the wall. At the end of the attic, one of Henry's doors was open, and the light reached into the shadows and rested on a single bare foot. Once again, Henry had fallen asleep with his light on. Only this time it wasn't so much falling asleep as it was collapsing across his bed as sleep dragged him down.

You're falling, the light whispered to the foot.

Henry jerked, kicked the other door open, and sat up. He squinted at the daylight and then looked at the wall behind him. Plaster still hung in the corners near the ceiling, and behind his bed by the floor. But in a circle surrounding the compass locks the wall was clear. All of it was made up of small cupboard doors.

Henry stood up and headed for the stairs. He was probably in trouble. Plaster rubble was all over his room and clung to his hands and arms. He could taste it in his mouth, his sinuses felt packed with the stuff, and his eyes itched. And it was already morning. Everyone was probably up, and it would be impossible for him to hide what he'd been doing when he walked downstairs looking like something fossilized in plaster and dust.

Standing at the top of his stairs, Henry could hear the dining room clock ticking, but nothing else. He stepped onto the top stair. It whined, but not too loudly. Breathing out, he took another step. He was expecting a slow creak, a pop, or even a crackle. He was not expecting a sharp piece of plaster.

As Henry jumped back, his heel caught the stair. His other foot slipped. He landed on his shoulder blades, hitting his head and sliding to the bottom in a cloud of gray dust. He gasped, sure he was dead or at least paralyzed, but he could feel his toes throbbing. He jumped up and ran straight into the bathroom.

Henrietta and Aunt Dotty, the only two who were roused by Henry's rumbling descent, stepped out of their rooms and into the thin cloud of dust still floating down the attic stairs and settling on the green carpet. The shower turned on.

"Back to bed, Henrietta," Dotty said. "Your cousin needs a clock." She yawned, and the two shuffled back to their rooms.

* * *

Henry stood in the shower and watched a sandbar form below him. He kicked at it and smeared it with his feet until he'd forced it down the drain. When he was done, he scurried back up to the attic in a towel, his arms full of his filthy clothes.

He stood in his doorway and assessed his room. His bed was almost completely hidden beneath chunks of plaster, big and small, while the floor looked like a cross between a beach and a gravel driveway. Dust was everywhere—all over his lamp, the walls, the inside of his doors, and even the floor a few feet outside his bedroom doors. He really had no idea how he was going to clean the mess up, but at the moment he didn't care. He was staring at his wall.

At the very first, when he had only just found the second door, he'd assumed the wall was some sort of built-in cabinet. But the second door was a very pale wood, almost white, completely different from the first door. He didn't know what kind of wood it was, but then, nobody in Kansas would have. There were only two people alive who would recognize the wood in that door. One was a man living in a run-down apartment in a bad part of Orlando. He would have recognized it and then tried to find something strong to drink, because he very much wanted to believe that most of his childhood had not actually happened.

The other was an old woman in France. Her

husband had returned from the First World War with some very strange stories and a small sapling in a tin cup. He had told her its name then, and the name of the man who had given it to him, and she had never forgotten either. The tree is in her backyard garden now, squat and strong, and before her husband died, years ago, he made her a jewelry box out of one of its limbs that had been torn off in a storm.

Henry did not know these people. He had looked at the small wooden door with its pale grain and silver-lined keyhole, and he had dragged his fingers across it, unable to read the story the wood told. "What are you?" he'd asked out loud.

Henry had continued chipping plaster and un-covering doors until he could count thirty-five in all, and he had no doubt there were more. Most of them were wood, but of all different sizes, grains, and colors. The shapes varied as well as the designs. Some were plain, and some had surfaces so intricately carved that getting the plaster out of all the curves and crannies had been impossible. Some had knobs, some small handles, some slides or things Henry had never seen. There was one with nothing at all. He had pushed and pulled and lightly thumped on every single one, but without effect. And then, always, he had gone back to chipping plaster, making his newly sharpened knife dull and duller. A large blister now crowned his thumb from pushing on the blade to keep it open, and the knuckles on both of his hands were missing skin.

Henry tiptoed through the rubble and dug some clothes out of the crammed drawers in his dresser. He pulled them on and then went down to the kitchen to find the broom and dustpan. He also saw the clock in the dining room and realized why nobody was up. He swept all the dust and gravel off his floor and the floor of the attic and once again dumped it onto his blanket. He cleaned off his walls, his lamp, his dresser, and his nightstand. No matter how much he swept, there was some dust so fine that it only scurried away from the broom and drifted into the air.

Eventually he gave up on the finer stuff, moved his antique Kansas basketball poster to cover part of what he had done to the wall, wondered where he could get more posters, and grabbed the corners of his blanket to carry it out to the side of the barn.

He dragged the makeshift sack to the stairs and began lugging it down, one stair at a time. He had not realized how heavy it would be. By the time he had reached the fourth stair, he was sweating, and every time he moved his blanket, dust swirled out and clung to his skin. When he reached the bottom of the second flight of stairs, he was in pain. In the mudroom, he sat down to catch his breath and put on his shoes.

When Henry finally reached the barn, he turned to

look back at the house. He had plowed an obvious trail through the tall grass with his sack of plaster, but there was nothing he could do about it now. He looked at the small pile of plaster he had dumped the night before and compared it to the size of his new sack. He was going to have to go farther from the house.

Rather than drag his sack through the even-taller grass and weeds that led to the fields behind the barn, he buckled down, hoisted the blanket over his shoulder, and staggered off. He didn't know how far he should take it, but he figured he wouldn't be able to carry it for very long and would dump it when he stopped.

The grass beyond the barn rubbed against his elbows as he moved through it. Then the tall grass ended, and there, at his feet, was an old irrigation ditch. Henry dropped the blanket, grabbed two of the corners, and watched his demolition work slide down the bank into the still water. Then he sat. He was sweating, and now that he wasn't moving anymore, his sweat made him cold in the slight morning breeze. He lay back into the tall grass, ducking under the moving air, and was warm. The sun played around in the tops of the weeds, pointing out the seeds they carried high and, in them, a villainous intent to fill the Earth.

Exhaustion crawled out of Henry's bones, and he slept.

* * *

If water bugs could see more than a yard, then several of them would have noticed the bottoms of Henry's feet and the legs of his pants. Such far-sighted bugs would have had a much better view of Uncle Frank. He was sitting next to Henry's knees with his legs stretched down the bank into the ditch. In his right hand he held a wooden baseball bat, and with his left he searched the bank for pieces of plaster. When he found them, he tossed them gently into the air, where he either hit them across the ditch with the bat or missed and watched them hop down the bank and into the water. Occasionally he looked at Henry's face. Dotty had told him how early Henry had been up and how he'd begun his day on the stairs. Frank's job had been to find Henry, and now he had.

Frank Willis was a thoughtful man, even if he didn't always look it. As he sat and tossed bits of plaster, he was thinking. Most people from Henry, Kansas, the ones who thought he was thin, would have assumed his thoughts were limited to the things directly in front of him. They would have assumed he was thinking about his nephew, a filthy blanket, and bits of plaster scattered down the bank and gathered in the water at the bottom of the ditch.

Frank had noticed these things, but they only made him think of another summer, the summer when he first tumbled into Henry, Kansas—when he had tumbled in and never tumbled out. Only a year or two older than his nephew was now, he had propped himself up beside this same irrigation ditch beside this same barn. He had looked out over the sprawling landscape and smooth sky and wondered where exactly he was supposed to be.

Henry twisted in his sleep, and his foot slid down toward the still water.

"Henry," Frank said. "Wake up, boy." He reached over and shook him by the shoulder.

Henry woke up with a twitch and blinked at his uncle. Uncle Frank held up a piece of plaster between his finger and thumb, smiled, tossed the plaster in the air, and missed it with the bat.

"Bad dream, Henry?" he asked. "You didn't seem to be enjoying it too much, so I roused you."

Henry watched Uncle Frank pick up another chunk of plaster. This time he hit it well into the field on the other side of the ditch.

"Yeah," Henry said. "Not so much a bad dream. More a weird one."

"You like it out here by the fields?" Frank asked.

Henry nodded.

"So do I," Frank said. "Helps me think." Frank looked over at him. "You know, Henry, I've gained some worldly wisdom since we last spoke of tumblin' weeds." He raised his eyebrows. "I used to think a Japanese businessman and his money were soon parted. Now I've learned different. It's only true if you're from Texas."

"What do you mean?"

"Well, just an hour or two after the auction closed on my tumbleweed, some guy piles on there sellin' 'Genuine Texas Tumbleweed.' He throws in a certificate of authenticity and a little framed photo of the weed where he found it. My buyers backed out and bought his stuff."

"Oh, I'm sorry, Uncle Frank." Henry glanced at the blanket and the plaster and then looked quickly back at his uncle. "What're you going to do with all the tumbleweed in the barn?"

"Set it free." Frank sighed. "It's wild stuff anyway. Wasn't meant to live in captivity. My heart breaks to see it in a cage and all that." Three straight plaster chunks floated into the air. Frank only missed the last one.

"Do we have to take it back?" Henry asked. "Back to the culverts?"

"Nope. I'll just throw it in the yard. The wind'll do what it always does, and the weeds will tumble until the world does what it does and they all drop into another culvert."

Frank braced himself with the bat and clambered to his feet. Henry followed him.

"Or maybe they'll roll free for a while," Frank said. "I'd like to think they could see some things, make a few pilgrimages before they settle." He turned and faced Henry. "Well, we got a busy afternoon ahead of us, so we better loosen up and head back."

"What do we have to do?" Henry asked.

"I sharpened your knife up a bit last night, but I wanted to put a little better edge on it." Frank held the bat up. "And I dug this out of the barn so we could play some baseball." He stepped off through the tall grass. "And don't forget your blanket," he said over his shoulder. "You might want to shake it out. It's lookin' pretty gritty."

Henry did shake out his blanket, then nervously followed Uncle Frank back toward the barn.

"Heard you fell down the stairs this morning, Henry," Uncle Frank said. "You don't seem too much worse for wear. I've been down those myself. Only I broke my collarbone."

"Yeah," Henry said. "It was early. I thought I'd slept in again."

"Oh, don't worry about that," Uncle Frank said. "Boys should sleep in during the summer. I don't know how else people expect them to grow. Dots says I got to get you a clock for your room, though. I don't think I have anything in the barn. Not anything that works. We'll see if she asks again."

Frank began whistling, glanced back again to make sure Henry was far enough behind, and then swung the bat through the grass. The barn loomed beside them.

"Do you have any more old posters, Uncle Frank?" Henry asked. He was trying not to sound guilty. "In the barn, I mean? That I could hang up in my room?"

Frank stuck his lower lip up toward his nose while he walked. "Not sure. I'll look around, though." He stopped at the back door. "Let's start with your knife. We'll take a little batting practice after lunch. Where is your knife? You must have grabbed it, because I left it on the counter."

"Yeah, it's up in my room. I'll get it for you." Henry ran around his uncle, kicked off his shoes in the mudroom, and scrambled up both flights of stairs. In his room, he threw his blanket back onto his bed, kicked his filthy clothes from the night before underneath, grabbed his knife off his dresser, and then hurried back down. He found Uncle Frank sitting at the dining room table.

"Don't know why a boy shouldn't run," Frank was saying. "He's just excited to get his knife sharp." He was unrolling an old cloth. Aunt Dotty stepped in from the living room. She smiled.

"Careful, Henry. You won't have much knife left

when he's done, and he's not too good at straight lines." She ducked away before Frank could answer.

"It'll be sharp!" he yelled after her. "Don't know what she's complainin' about. Okay, Henry, fork it over." Henry did, and Uncle Frank examined it.

"Tell you the truth, Henry," he said, "I don't know why I ever bought you this knife."

Henry's heart sank. He had thought it was impossible for his uncle not to be suspicious about his blanket and all the plaster, and now trouble had finally come.

"It's worthless," Frank continued. "The blade's already down to a nub and the tip's broke off. I can still sharpen her up for you, but you need a new one. You take off and do whatever you wanna do. This will take me a little while. I'll holler when I'm done."

"Your cousins are playing out in the barn if you like," Dotty said from the living room, and the vacuum growled to life.

"Thanks!" Henry yelled. But he went upstairs to his room. When he got there, he found Henrietta kneeling on his bed, looking at the wall. Her hair was pulled back into a tight braid.

"I took the poster down already," she said. "I hope you don't mind." She glanced back at him and her smile was wide. She looked different without her thick curls, smaller even. Henry watched her put both hands on the wall and run them over the doors. "What are they all for?" she asked.

"Probably to put things in," Henry said. "I mean exciting things," he added.

Henry flopped down beside her, and the two of them stared at the little cupboard doors.

"How many more do you think there are?" Henrietta asked.

"I bet they cover the whole wall," Henry said.

"You tried to open every one?" She reached out and wiggled a knob.

Henry nodded. "I did. I wrecked my knife getting the plaster off last night, and I won't be able to use it tonight because your dad is sharpening it again. He'll wonder if it's dull again tomorrow."

Henrietta looked at him. "There are some old tools in the basement, and some more in the barn. I bet there's a chisel. Do you want me to check?"

"That would be good," Henry said. "It took me forever last night. I kept worrying that I was scratching the doors. I hope we don't mess any of them up."

"I like the white one best," Henrietta said, and pointed. "It looks happiest. Some of the other ones don't seem to want to be here, but the white one seems just fine."

"What do you mean?" Henry sat up straight. "I think it looks neat, too, but how could it look happier than the others? I don't think you can call them happy."

"Well, what about sad? That little metal one looks sad." And she pointed again. It was the smallest door Henry had uncovered, no more than four inches tall by five inches wide, with a keyhole on the left side. Its metal surface was grooved and still held bits of plaster. A small black panel was inset toward the bottom.

"I don't think it looks sad at all," Henry said. "It's been stuck in the wall for however long. It's probably glad to be out again."

"I don't think it wants to be in our attic," Henrietta said. "It looks like it's supposed to be somewhere else. What do you think the black part's made of?" She leaned forward and picked at it with her fingernail. "I think it's plastic."

"What?" Henry stuck his finger beside Henrietta's. "Plastic's not that old, is it?" He scratched and felt something pile up against his fingertip. "Oh," he said, and sat back up.

"What? What is it?" Henrietta grabbed at his finger to look at it.

"I think it's paint," Henry said, picking the black out from beneath his nail. He looked back at the little panel in the door. "It must be glass that someone painted over."

"Really?" Henrietta began scratching at the panel with both hands. "We could see through it with a flashlight."

"Henry?" Aunt Dotty's voice drifted up two flights of stairs. "Your lunch is ready. Come on down. Henrietta, you, too, if you're up there."

Henrietta sat up quickly.

"Can we just pretend like we didn't hear?" Henry asked.

"No. Then she'll just come up. Let's go. We can do it later." Henrietta stood up and pulled Henry to his feet.

"Henry!"

"We're coming, Mom!" Henrietta yelled, and the two of them thumped down the stairs. Henrietta stopped suddenly, and Henry bumped into her. She bent over and picked up a piece of plaster off a stair. She looked up and down the entire flight and made a face at Henry. "Mom will notice," she said.

Anastasia and Penelope were already eating when they got there. Uncle Frank sat between them, working Henry's knife across a stone. Two plates of grilled cheese and two glasses of milk sat across the table from the girls.

"What have you been doing, Henrietta?" Anastasia asked, chewing. "I thought you said you were gonna come back out and play."

"I did," Henrietta said as she and Henry sat down. "But I saw Henry and we started talking."

"What about?" Anastasia asked. "Zeke Johnson?" She picked at a lump of cheese between the bread crusts, stretching it into a string.

Henrietta glared at Anastasia.

"You're being rude," Penelope said.

"I'm not," Anastasia said. "She said she was coming back, and I just want to know what they talked about. You two always talk about Zeke."

"Girls," Uncle Frank said, "I don't think it matters. You can all play after lunch."

Henry looked at Henrietta. Her jaw was locked shut. Penelope was red.

"We were talking about lost doors and secret cities and how to find them," Henry said, and he took a bite of his sandwich.

"Fun," Penelope said. "I found a secret door in the bathroom once."

"What you found," Aunt Dotty said, entering from the kitchen with Frank's sandwich, "was a bunch of mouse droppings."

"And—listen, Henry," Penelope said. "Mouse droppings

and a shower mat. You know those rubber things with all the suction circles on the bottom? There was one of those."

"So what did you do with it?" Henry asked.

"Set traps for the mice and closed it back up," Uncle Frank said.

"I can show it to you," Penelope offered. "If Dad will let me take it back off."

"Nope!" Dotty yelled from the kitchen. "I don't want you breaking the paint all up again. There's a more important door your uncle can show you, Henry. It's much harder to get open than the bathroom panel." She walked into the room, drying a skillet with a rag. "Frank, I ran into Gladys and Billy at the store yesterday. Do you know what he said to me?"

The girls went very quiet. Frank didn't look up.

"Hello?" he asked, and kept rubbing Henry's knife.

Dotty hit him with her rag. "He said that. And so did she. But the important part was when he said, 'Frank ever get that door open?' Do you know what I said? What I said was— Are you ready for this? I said, 'No.' "

"Ah," Frank said. He lifted Henry's knife up to his mouth and dabbed the blade with his tongue. "That's my honest wife. I appreciate you lookin' out for my dignity."

"And then I said I would give him a call to come by

and open it. I'd rather not be a liar, Frank." She crossed her arms. The skillet dangled on one hip, the rag on the other.

"Dots, excellent wife, I appreciate that. I'll get that door open and accommodate you spaciously within the room hidin' behind it. But Billy Mortensen will have nothing to do with it. He threw a baseball game in the state playoffs our senior year, and you know it." Frank glanced up. "I'll only see him socially. He'll never bill me."

"We could pay up front," Dotty said, and walked back into the kitchen.

The sounds of metal scratching on flint and slowly chewed grilled cheese dominated the room. Finally, Frank set Henry's knife down, ate his sandwich in two bites, and drained his milk. He stood and put his hands on his hips.

"Women and children behind the lines!" he yelled, and all the girls jumped. Henry froze with his mouth open. "Bang the drum slowly and ask not for whom the bell's ringing, for the answer's unfriendly!" He threw a fist in the air. "Two years have my black ships sat before Troy, and today its gate shall open before the strength of my arm." Dotty was laughing from the kitchen. Frank looked at his nephew. "Henry, we play baseball tomorrow. Today we sack cities. Dots! Fetch me my tools! Down with the French! Once more into the breach, and fill the wall with our coward dead! Half a league! Half a league! Hey, batter, batter!"

Frank brought his fist down onto the table, spilling Anastasia's milk, and then he struck a pose with both arms above his head and his chin on his chest. The girls cheered and applauded. Aunt Dotty stepped back into the dining room carrying a red metal toolbox.

Frank sniffed. "You know me well, wife. I thought those were in the basement."

"They were. You should have been an English teacher, Frank."

"What are we going to do?" Henry asked.

"We're going to build a wooden horse, stick you inside it, and offer it up as a gift," Frank answered.

"Burn your bridges when you come to them," Dotty said. She smiled at Frank, picked up the empty plates, and walked back into the kitchen.

"Can we watch?" Henrietta asked.

"You," Frank said, "can go play in the barn, the yard, the fields, or the ditches, so long as you are nowhere near the action. C'mon, Henry."

The girls moaned and complained while Henry followed his uncle up the stairs. At the top, they walked all the way around the landing until they faced the very old, very wooden door to Grandfather's bedroom. Uncle Frank set down his tools.

"Today is the day, Henry. I can feel it. I never told your aunt this, but my favorite book's in there. I was reading it to your grandfather near the end. It's been due back at the library for a while now, and it'd be nice to be able to check something else out."

CHAPTER FIVE

Henry sat on the floor of the landing and watched his uncle fiddle with the doorknob.

"Here it comes," Uncle Frank said, and pulled. The knob rattled off in Frank's hand.

"What's that spike thing?" Henry asked.

"That, Henry, is the spike thing that sticks through the door and holds the knob things." He looked at Henry and waggled his eyebrows. "Now we're gonna be a little more gutsy than I have been in the past. She's waited two years, and I figure she's been patient enough." Frank put his thumb on the end of the protruding spike and pushed. It herked and jerked a bit but went all the way into the door. When it was behind the old brass cover plate, Uncle Frank used a screwdriver to push it the rest of the way through. Henry heard a thump on the other side of the door.

"That's the knob droppin' on the other side," Uncle Frank said. "We aren't puttin' it back on unless we get the door open. I'll tell you something, Henry. Today

I'm gonna do something I've resisted doing for two years. If the door won't open, we're gonna bash it in. It's a nice old door, not many like it around anymore. I'd hate to bust it up, but it'll probably be the jamb that splits."

"Do you think it will open?" Henry asked.

"Nope," Frank said. "But I'm not going downstairs with my head hangin'. I'll poke and prod the insides a bit, then I'll start kickin'."

The poking and prodding lasted about forty-five minutes. The cover plate came off. Everything that Frank could get at came off. Screwdrivers stabbed and twisted. Finally, Uncle Frank stood, put his hands on his lower back, leaned backward, and rocked to the sides. The cat walked past Henry and rubbed itself on Frank's leg.

"Well, here we go. Lord forgive me." Frank raised his right foot and kicked hard against the door just where the knob had been. There was a scream downstairs.

"Is it open?" Dotty yelled.

"Quiet, woman!" Frank yelled back. "Soon will be." He kicked again. The door didn't budge, but it made an enormous sound, like a huge wooden drum.

Frank backed up as much as the landing would allow, took five quick steps, and jumped at the door. His body piled into it, and then piled onto the floor. The cat, who had been observing from the corner, strolled away. Henry didn't say anything. He tried to keep on not saying anything. And then he laughed. Frank began laughing as well but quickly stopped himself.

"Got to get this thing open," he said. "I have never seen an oak door this solid, and this one's fir."

"Fir? Is fir like pine?" Henry asked. "I thought pine was soft."

"It is. Fir's a bit different, but not this different." Frank examined the wood of the door. "Looks like fir. Grain might be a little funny, but still fir. Look out, Henry, I'm gonna try to hurt myself again. Then we'll get drastic."

Henry scooted farther back.

"Seen this in a movie once," Uncle Frank said. He rocked in place, then took four steps and jumped. He put his feet out in front of him and leaned back. When his feet hit the door, he fell backward and landed hard, flat on his back with his legs up the door. He was gasping.

"Are you okay, Uncle Frank?" Henry asked. "Should I get Aunt Dotty?"

"No," Uncle Frank gasped. "Just my wind. Knocked out." He sat up slowly, then stood. "You wait here. I'll be right back. Got to be a bit sneaky." He put his finger to his lips, then crept down the stairs.

After a moment, Henry heard his aunt Dotty's voice.

"Frank? What are you doing?"

"Just grabbin' a few more tools. Back in a minute."

"How's it going?"

"Not too bad."

Henry heard the back door slam. He was alone with his thoughts and the cat, who had reappeared and was now cleaning himself at the other end of the landing. Henry looked at the cat. The cat looked at him.

"Sorry about that whole thing last time," Henry said. The cat looked him over, then went back to collecting hair with its tongue.

Henry sat on the green-carpeted landing for five minutes. He finally grew impatient and stood to go up to his room. At the same moment, Uncle Frank rose out of the stairwell holding an ax. The head was all rust and a little red paint, but the edge looked sharp. Henry wondered when his uncle had last used it. Or if he just kept it on a regular sharpening schedule, like Aunt Dotty's knives.

Frank gripped the ax handle and laughed. "Here we are, Henry. We've grown serious." Henry stepped out of the way as Frank approached the door. His uncle reached up to his neck and fished out a black string from inside his shirt. A silver ring dangled at the end.

Frank kissed it quickly and tucked it back into his shirt. As he turned his hips, his right hand slid to the top of the ax handle and his left dropped to the bottom. He shifted his weight from foot to foot and tipped his head from side to side. It was obvious to Henry that while Frank may have been out of ax practice, he had once done it a great deal and enjoyed it immensely.

Frank swung, his hips squaring and his right hand sliding down the handle to meet his left.

Grandfather's door had once been a normal fir. It had four panels: two large vertical rectangles at the top and two smaller ones at the bottom. Its stain was dark, like walnut, but there was a lot of red buried beneath it. The color would pull the eyes and then duck and run, calling for them to try and find it. Eyes never could. But they knew it was there somewhere.

There are places where whole forests of trees have been petrified and turned to stone. Usually this happens at the bottoms of lakes after volcanic eruptions. Grandfather's door had not been petrified, and it was not stone. But it was something very close. Its core was stronger than stone because it was less brittle. Frank's ax might have cracked a petrified door, but not Grandfather's.

The ax blade rattled the wood and ricocheted back.

Frank leaned the ax against the wall, shook his hands, and examined the mark he had made. He had struck in the groove beside the top panel on the right side of the door. It was as thin as any part of the door, and the ax should have broken right through. Instead, the notch left by his swing was no more than an eighth of an inch deep. Frank didn't say anything. He didn't look at Henry. He grabbed the ax and began swinging.

Henry watched blow after blow bounce off the door. Left and right Frank swung, always along the edges of the panels. The ax hopped and skipped, slid and twisted. Breathing heavily, Frank finally stopped and wiped the sweat from his head. There were small slivers of wood all over the carpet.

"Henry," he said between gasps. "I'm not sure this will work." He picked up the ax and ran his finger along its blade. "Dull already," he muttered.

"Are we giving up?" Henry asked.

"Nope. We're going to a barbeque tonight. I told Dots that one way or another, it'd be open before we left. You can run do whatever. I've gotta think on this for a bit."

"Are you sure? Do you need me to do anything?"

"Nope. Scram." Henry went to Grandfather's door and felt it with his hands. The notches were shallow, but there were a lot of them.

"Why doesn't the ax work?"

"Dunno. That's what I gotta think on. Your grandpa was a weird one, just as selfish dead as alive, but this is stranger than anything. Run on now. I'm headin' out to the barn. You'll hear me when I'm back if you wanna watch my last stand." With that, Frank wandered back downstairs with the blunt ax over his shoulder.

Henry did not hold still for long. Once his uncle was out of sight, he scrambled up the attic stairs and immediately applied his fingernails to the paint on the small door. A moment later, he hopped off his bed and ran down both flights of stairs before walking calmly to the dining room table, where he retrieved his newly sharpened knife. Then he reversed direction and hurried back to his room.

Sitting on his bed, Henry examined the new edge on his now-much-smaller knife blade. Frank had taken at least a third of the blade off, but it really was sharp. Henry was a little afraid to touch it. Still, he rubbed his thumb across the blade and knew that what he held was truly dangerous. It looked at Henry's fingers in an insinuating way, as if to say, "You wouldn't be the first. Why do you think they got rid of me?" The edge, as Dotty had warned, was not straight. Nor was the curve of the blade consistent. It was frozen in a ripple, like the surface of a windy lake.

Henry bent down and scraped at the paint with his knife. It came off easily but in very narrow strips. It was not a large area, only an inch or so high and about three wide, but it took him a while. When the paint was finally off, the glass still did not look like anything you would be able to see through.

Henry had put down his knife, cupped his hands over the glass, and was staring intently into complete lightlessness when he heard feet on the attic stairs. He knew it had to be Henrietta, but he still jumped and was outside of his room with the doors shut by the time she reached the top. She was lugging a cardboard box under one arm.

"Hi," she said, smiling. "I brought a bunch of posters from the barn. Dad had a box he forgot about. They're all the same basketball guy, and they say 'University of Kansas, National Champions' even though Dad says they weren't that year. He thought he could sell them to people in England who wouldn't know better, but they didn't want them, so he says you can have them all. I brought tape, too, and a chisel. Why couldn't Dad get Grandpa's door open? Did you get the paint off?"

She dropped the box of posters on the floor.

"I stuck the chisel in the bottom."

"Thanks," Henry said. "I got the paint off, but I still can't see anything. It's all smeary."

They went into his room, and Henrietta examined the small door.

"I think it's a mailbox," she said.

"What do you mean a mailbox?" Henry ran his fingers over the grooves in the little door. "It doesn't look anything like a mailbox."

"The kind in post offices," Henrietta said. "I used to go to the post office with Mom sometimes, and there are little boxes like this there."

"You mean post office boxes?" Henry prodded the glass with his knife. "Why would there be a post office box in my bedroom?"

Henrietta laughed. "Why would any of these be in your bedroom?"

"I don't know," Henry said. "I guess someone could have just been a sort of collector. You know, of little things with doors. They must have just liked cupboards."

"No," Henrietta said. "It has to be more exciting than that." Henrietta sat up on the bed and crossed her legs. "Somebody hid them all, so they're supposed to be secret. We have to get them open and find out why."

"Do you think we'll ever be able to see through this little one?" Henry cupped his hands against the small door and peered in. Henrietta pushed him out of the way. She licked and slobbered all over the ends of her fingers and then rubbed them on the glass. Then she pulled her sleeve down over her hand and wiped it clean.

Henry looked in again. "It's clear enough," he said, "but I still can't see anything. We need a flashlight."

"I've got one in my room." Henrietta jumped up. It didn't take her long to get it, and when she came back in, she closed both doors tight behind her and stepped over to Henry's reading light. When she turned it off, the room was near pitch. Except for the trickle of daylight that filtered beneath the doors, there was no light at all.

Henry tried not to shiver. This wasn't make-believe. He really had found these doors, and he didn't know what was inside them. He suddenly wondered why something hidden inside a secret cupboard would have to be pleasant.

Henrietta flipped on her flashlight and handed it to him.

"Take it," she said. "Look in the door. You found it."

Henry took it. He knelt on his bed, put the flashlight beside his right eye, and, swallowing hard, he looked.

"I think I can see something." He shifted his head. "It looks like an envelope." He handed the flashlight to Henrietta and knee-waddled out of her way. She bent and looked.

"It looks skinnier than an envelope," she said. "Maybe a postcard."

Henry leaned his hand against the wall and bent over to look.

"Move your head a bit," he said. She did, and he looked again, bracing himself against the cupboard wall. He was holding on to something metal. It slid, and he fell over onto Henrietta. She screamed. They both fell off the bed. Above them, a cupboard door banged against the wall.

Henry lay still, all of his senses straining. The flashlight was off. His eyes hurt, they were open so wide. He could make out Henrietta on the floor by the light from the door. He could smell something big and feel a cold wind on his skin. He could hear rustling, and Henrietta holding back tears. He could taste fear in the back of his throat, constricted to the point of pain.

Henry had never thought of himself as brave. He never had been. What he did next wasn't a terrific act of bravery, but it did take effort. With every inch of his skin crawling at the touch of cold, moving air, he sat up, found his way to the head of his bed, and turned on his light. The cupboard door just above the post office box was open and swinging gently back and forth, lightly tapping the wall, then almost closing.

He looked at Henrietta. She looked back at him, her face white and eyes wide.

"Are you okay?" he whispered.

"What is it doing?" she asked.

Henry reached up and held his hand in front of the moving door. "There's air coming through it."

They both held still for a moment, listening.

"Can you hear that?" she asked. "What is it?"

"It sounds like trees blowing around," Henry said.

"Should we look inside?" Henrietta asked. Henry climbed onto his bed. A cool wind pushed around his face and through his hair as it came out of the cupboard. Henry held the door still.

Henrietta climbed up beside him.

"There's something inside. On the bottom," Henry said. He stretched out his hand. He could barely see what he was reaching for. It was simply a shape. His hand felt something and closed. It was a string. He pulled the string out of the cupboard. Dangling below his fingers was a small key.

The wind blowing out of the cupboard suddenly became a gust. Henry's bedroom doors blew open, and dust shuffled and rolled across the floor toward the attic window. The noise of the trees roared like a waterfall. The two of them could hear boughs bending and creaking. Then they smelled it, sudden and fresh. Somewhere on the other side of the cupboard, rain had begun to fall.

"Shut it quick," Henrietta said. "Mom and Dad will hear it. They'll *feel* it."

Henry pushed the door closed on the wind. Then he slid the metal latch, and the room was quiet.

"How did you get it unlocked?" Henrietta asked.

"I don't think it *was* locked," Henry said. "It must have just been stuck. I leaned on it to look through the glass, and it came open."

Henrietta's hair was coming loose in the front. She brushed it back and put her eyebrows up. "It's magic," she said. "We can't pretend it's not. It's a magic cupboard. They're probably all magic."

Henry shifted on the bed and looked away. "I don't think it's magic," he said. "I think it's just something really unusual."

"Henry," Henrietta said. She leaned forward and spoke slowly. "It's not raining outside, and we don't have any trees back there."

"I know," Henry said. "I just think it's something like Quantum."

"What's Quantum?" Henrietta asked.

"Well," Henry said, "my dad says it's when things can sometimes be where they aren't, or two places at once."

"Sounds like magic."

"No, it's natural," Henry said. He was rocking nervously. "It just happens."

"You couldn't make something Quantum?" Henrietta asked.

"It's only for really little things."

"The cupboard's little."

"No," Henry said. "Really little. And trees and rain and wind aren't little."

"Okay. They're too big to be Quantum," Henrietta said. "So it has to be magic."

Henry wasn't sure what to say. He would have liked to discover that the whole thing was just some sort of trick, that he wouldn't really be sleeping beside a bunch of magic cupboards, but he didn't know any other way to explain what had just happened.

"I don't know," he finally said.

Henrietta shivered suddenly, bounced up on her knees, and focused her wide eyes on Henry. "Aren't you excited to see what's behind the other doors? There could be all sorts of things!"

Henry sat very still. "Aren't you scared at all?" he asked. "I mean, we might find something bad."

"Everybody always finds bad things," she said. "And things only get hidden like this if they're really bad or really good." She bounced again. "We'll just have to find out."

"I don't know," Henry said again. Despite his concerns, he was truly curious about the cupboards. He knew that if they got another one open, he would be terrified. But he would be sick with himself if he didn't try.

"Do you think the key opens another one?"

Henrietta pointed to it. Henry looked down at the

key in his hand. He was about to say "I don't know" for the third time when a rumbling, motorcycle-sounding engine fired up at the bottom of his stairs. Shoving the key in his pocket, he and Henrietta scrambled down the stairs.

At the bottom, they found Uncle Frank wearing plastic goggles and standing in front of Grandfather's door with a chain saw. He began singing something, then braced himself and pulled the trigger. As a cloud of black smoke blew out the back of the saw, the chain blade spun into loud motion. He leaned the blade back and slowly lowered it onto the door. When it touched, wood chips began flying all over the landing. It looked like Frank was fighting to keep the blade from sliding. It began to skid, and Frank spread his legs a little more. Then the saw caught on something and kicked back. The full force of the spinning chain threw Frank against the wall. He jumped as the saw, barely in his left hand, swung down toward his legs. It didn't hit them, but its nose caught the floor. In one short second, the saw dug itself in, shredding and wrapping long strands of green carpet around itself. There, nestled cozily into the floor, it idled. Panting, Frank reached down and turned off the engine.

Dotty was at the top of the stairs. She looked at Frank, then at the saw burrowed into the landing. She looked at Frank again.

"Time to go," she said. "We're due at the barbeque. You okay, Frank?"

Frank rubbed his cheek on his arm. "My pride's on the lower end," he said. "Floor's a bit dinged." He reached down and pulled at the quiet saw. It wouldn't budge. "I'll cut it out later, Dots. Sorry about . . . um." He sighed and put his hands on his head. "I figure I'll have to go through the bathroom wall."

"Mr. Willis," Aunt Dotty said, "I'm not sure if the house will survive you. Now, I think you need a hot dog." Frank seemed relieved. "C'mon, kids," Dotty added. "We're gonna be late for the barbeque."

Henry and Henrietta followed her down the stairs, glancing back at Grandfather's door and the saw. Frank came behind, still wearing his goggles. There were wood chips in his hair.

CHAPTER SIX

Henry stood with his back against the fence and watched the boys play. His emotions were mixed. In one sense, he was enjoying himself. Since arriving at the barbeque, he had consumed three generic colas. Now he was working on a root beer. He had never before consumed any sort of soda. He had seen commercials occasionally, which his father had told him were crass and capitalistic. Thus far, soda pleased him. But Henry's happiness was tempered by worry. What he was watching, while nursing his can of root beer, was baseball.

The grown-ups were all inside the yard, standing around grills or setting out casseroles, paper plates, and flimsy plastic utensils designed to snap when used. Henry's cousins had all disappeared into the front yard, and the boys had run out behind the house into a vacant lot with an old foundation to play baseball. They had enough foresight to bat away from the house toward the raggedy old trees, the street, and, beyond that, an abandoned warehouse squatting in the shadow of a rusty water tower. Not one hit had reached the street in the air, and balls hit on the ground died fast in the grip of the overgrown grass.

Henry was worried about the boys. He wasn't worried they might exclude him. He wasn't worried they might be too embarrassed to ask the new kid to play. He was worried that they might want him to. But no one had asked him yet, so he leaned against the fence, trying not to be too noticeable, drinking his root beer, and watching other boys run, pitch, throw, and try to hit.

"Your arm hurtin' you?" a voice behind him asked. Henry looked up into Frank's face.

"My arm?" Henry asked.

"Well, you aren't out there playin'. I thought it might be your wrist or your elbow."

"No. I'm just not feeling up to it." Henry sipped his root beer.

"Oh well. I don't feel up to most things most times," Frank said. "I'm gonna grab a beverage, and then I'll come back and watch your game."

Frank's head disappeared behind the fence, and Henry turned back toward the field. A tall boy in a sweat-stained baseball hat with a fraying bill stood in front of him.

"Are you Henry?" he asked.

"Yeah," Henry said.

"I'm Zeke Johnson," he said. "D'you play?"

"Not much," Henry said.

"D'you wanna play?" Zeke nodded at the field.

Normally, Henry would have lied. Instead, he surprised himself. "I forgot my glove," he said.

"Borrow mine," said Zeke. "We'll play opposite."

"I'm a lefty."

"So am I."

Henry held his breath. "Okay," he said, and looked around for a place to set his root beer. Zeke took it out of his hand and put it on the fence. Then, with Henry's blood doing strange things in his veins and his breath catching in his throat, the two of them walked out onto the scraggly grass of the makeshift diamond. The other boys nodded at Henry or said hi. Henry nodded back but couldn't say anything. Zeke introduced him, then gave Henry his glove and sent him into right field.

Uncle Frank leaned on the fence, watching the boys and sipping his beer. A bigger man leaned up next to him. "Hey, Frank," he said. "Dotty says you wanted to talk to me about your door trouble."

Frank glanced at him. The man was tall and looked strong. His fleshy face smiled beneath a yellow cap with a concrete truck above the bill. "Hey, Billy," Frank said. "Dotty said that?"

"How long's it been stuck?" Billy asked.

Frank stared out into the field, lifted his beer, and

winced at the taste. "Two years," he finally said. "I tried choppin' it today. I tried chainsawin' it and just wrecked the floor. The door won't budge."

"Well," Billy said. "You want me to take a look?"

The two men stood silently, watching a small kid overbalance swinging.

"Needs to choke up on the bat," Frank said.

Billy nodded and spat. "And his eyes are all over the place. Everywhere but the ball."

Frank stood up and took a deep breath. "Okay, Billy. I need you to look at it now. And tell Dotty I said no. I don't know when I could pay you. She handles the money, and it might be months before I could sneak some."

Billy nodded. Henry's team was running in to bat as the two men set their drinks on the fence next to Henry's root beer and left to find Billy's truck.

Henry stood at the plate and watched the fat kid wind up. He couldn't believe he was doing this. The kid was throwing the ball as hard as he could. He'd almost hit Henry the first time, and Henry wasn't even wearing a helmet. One of the boys from Henry's team was on second, and there were two outs. The fat kid threw the ball—it was coming right at him. Henry wanted to duck or squat or something. Instead, he leaned back and brought his hands around. The ball cracked off the handle of the bat, and instantly Henry's hands burned.

"Run!" somebody yelled. Henry carried the bat with him for a few steps, then remembered to drop it. He didn't even look to see where the ball had gone. He was sure he would be out if he looked. When he hit the sweatshirt that was first base, he left one foot on the shirt and hopped forward with the other, trying to stop. Then he fell over.

"You can run through the bag," the first baseman said. Henry looked at the pitcher. The shortstop was throwing him the ball.

"Where did it go?" Henry asked the first baseman. "Where did I hit it?"

"Short left. Did it hurt your hands? You hit it with the handle."

"Yeah," Henry said. He stood up, unsure of how to hold himself. He rubbed his throbbing hands together and then crossed his arms. The other runner was on third. But he wasn't really on it. He was leading off, sliding sideways with bent knees. Henry uncrossed his arms and stepped off the sweatshirt, trying to watch the pitcher, the other runner, and the batter all at once.

The batter popped out, and Zeke threw Henry his glove as he headed in from center field. Henry ran back out into right field, almost hoping someone would hit it to him. But not quite.

*　　*　　*

Frank and Billy stood on the landing. Billy was holding his toolbox. Frank wiped sweat off of his forehead before he spoke.

"I got the chain saw stuck in the floor right before we left for the barbeque. Haven't had time to cut it out yet."

Billy licked his lips. Wood chips were scattered all over the landing and partway down the stairs. The door looked like it had been attacked by a herd of angry beavers. The chain saw still rested in its tangled carpet nest. Billy knelt beside the door.

"Some job, Frank," he said. "Should have called me sooner, and maybe you could have skipped the Vietnam approach."

He fished in his toolbox, pulled out something black and metallic, and began probing the old keyhole. Frank heard a click.

"Was that it?" he asked.

"Almost." Billy pulled out a second tool, and a moment later, there was another click.

"Now," Billy said. "Now it will open." He leaned on the door. He stood up and thumped his shoulder against it. He stepped back and kicked it.

"Goodness," he said. "Somebody weld a plate on the other side of this? It's not locked as far as I can tell. Should pop right open." He kicked it again.

"That's why I used the ax," Frank said. "Wish I could just find the key."

"Key wouldn't help you. It's as unlocked as any key would make it. Something else has got it shut."

"Oh, I don't know," Frank said. "Might be a different kind of key. It's sure a different kind of lock."

"It's the same kind of lock that's in all of these old houses," Billy said. "Nothing special about it."

They were silent again.

"I would have gone straight to the chain saw," Billy finally said. "What happened with it?"

"Kicked. Swung down and ate the carpet."

"Mind if I give it a try?"

"Gotta cut it out first." Frank pulled a knife from his pocket and flipped it open. He cut the strands of carpet away from the saw while Billy tried to pull it out. After a few wiggles and two big tugs, they got it free of the floor. Billy examined the chain.

"Bit dull," he said. "And full of carpet."

"Wasn't," Frank said. Billy pulled the starter cord, and the engine muttered. He pulled again, and the engine sounded irritated. A third pull roused it completely, and the landing filled with exhaust.

Billy stepped toward the door.

By the time Henry, his cousins, his aunt, and his uncle were all home and unloaded, Henry had consumed a total of six sodas of various types (four of them caffeinated), two sausages, and a hamburger. And he desperately needed to go to the bathroom.

Standing in front of the downstairs bathroom mirror, he reviewed his baseball accomplishments.

He had struck out twice, and hit one single and a double. His double had gone all the way to the trees. He had flubbed a fly ball in right field, but had fielded a grounder and thrown it almost all the way to second base. Zeke Johnson, though much bigger than Henry, wanted him to come over to hit sometime this week. Henry would be in Zeke's class in the fall.

Henry turned on the faucet and watched the water become brown as it ran over his hands. He could hear his cousins yelling and laughing. He wouldn't go to school in Kansas if his parents were back. Something knotted in his stomach. He felt horribly guilty. Only a few days in a new house, and he had already forgotten them. They were probably miserable.

But, he thought, it wasn't completely his fault for forgetting. Strange things had been distracting him. Of course he hoped they would be found and returned. But if that was going to happen, it was going to happen whether or not he worried about it. And he was playing baseball, and Zeke did want him to come to his house, and, most importantly, he needed to figure out what was going on in his bedroom.

Henry wandered into the living room, where his cousins were begging Uncle Frank to let them watch a movie. He thumped past them and up to his bedroom, trying to feel unhappy for his parents. When he got to the bottom of the attic stairs, he took one step up and stopped. Cold air was drifting down around him. He took two more slow steps, smelling and listening. The air smelled like grass and wet earth. He could hear trees.

The entire attic, normally the hottest place in the house, was extremely chilly. His two doors were open, and a quiet wind was crawling out of his bedroom and past him. The lights were off, but it wasn't completely dark outside, so he could just see the wall of his bedroom from where he stood. The cupboard door was open. He could hear trees gently moaning, creaking like ships, somewhere beyond his bed. When he stood just inside his doors, he looked carefully to both his left and right, then took another step and sogged into a puddle of very cold water. He jumped back, felt his way to his light, and turned it on.

The end of his bed beneath the open cupboard was soaking wet. An enormous puddle covered the floor, reaching almost to his doorway and filling the right side of the room. The cupboard door was swinging slightly, and all the doors beneath it, as well as the plaster, were drenched. Henry knelt on his bed, felt his mattress squelch beneath his knee, and looked in the cupboard. He could see nothing. But he could smell wet earth and thick, contented moss. He could hear leaves tossing in their sleep. He shut the door, slid the latch, and found a dry spot on his bed. Picking at the wet knee of his jeans, he looked at the water on his floor. There were three earthworms, big ones, swollen in the puddle.

"Worms," Henry said out loud. There were worms in a puddle on the floor in the attic.

Dotty and Frank stood in the kitchen sipping sun tea. The girls were watching something or other on television.

"What'd Billy say?" Dotty asked.

"What do you mean?" Frank asked. "I told you I wasn't going to ask him."

"But you did." Dotty smiled, brushed back her hair, and took a drink. Then she kissed him on the cheek. "Thanks for talking to him, Frank. I know you have your pride."

"My pride's why I asked him," Frank muttered. "He couldn't open it, either. Proved I didn't need him." He set his tea down. "I'm gonna blob with the girls."

Anastasia and Penelope were on the floor in front of the television. Frank plopped next to them.

"Henrietta went upstairs with Henry," Anastasia said. "She said we couldn't come."

"Did you want to go?" Frank asked.

"Yes," Anastasia said.

"No," Penelope said. "Henry's not very good at playing games. Henrietta is just being nice to him."

"I think they have a secret," Anastasia said.

"It's not nice to try and find out people's secrets," Penelope said.

"Secrets are for finding out. Dad, do you think they have a secret?"

"Why don't you ask them?" Frank said.

Anastasia was excited. "Can I? Do they have to answer?"

"No," Frank said. "No, they don't have to answer."

"Can I ask them now?"

"Sure. Penny and I will keep track of the television for you, won't we, Pen?"

Penelope just bit her lip as Anastasia ran to the stairs.

Anastasia reached the attic stairs, slowed down, and listened. She knew that the first step to asking about secrets is seeing how much you can find out by sneaking. She had been wanting to sneak for days. She had wanted to follow Henrietta when she got out of bed late the night before. Penelope hadn't let her. She wanted to spy on Henry in his room and go through his drawers, but Penelope wouldn't let her. Penelope thought it was more fun when people wanted to tell you things. Anastasia thought it was more fun to find out what they didn't want to tell you.

She could hear Henrietta's voice, though she couldn't tell what she was saying, and she could hear something slopping heavily on the floor. She could also hear tape being unrolled and torn across the teeth of its plastic holder. She spread her feet all the way against the walls on both sides of the stairs, put out her hands a few steps up, and began crawling.

"How do you think the latch came undone?" she heard Henrietta ask. "I saw you latch it. I know you didn't forget."

"I don't know," Henry said.

"It's a lot of water. You'll have to curl up on the dry end of your bed tonight."

"Yeah," Henry said. "I don't know if I'll sleep, though. I drank a lot of soda."

"So did I."

"I've never had soda before."

"What? You haven't?" Henrietta laughed. "Why not?"

"I think because it's bad for your teeth."

"Isn't everything bad for your teeth?"

"Probably."

"I think the worms are funny. It's weird that they came through."

"Yeah. I don't think they like my floor."

"Do you think the worms were Quantummed?"

"I don't know where they came from, but they'll probably like the backyard."

"I'm done with your wall. Should I put some on the ceiling?"

"Sure."

"What about the other wall?"

"Sure."

Henry was not thinking about what Henrietta was saying. He was slapping towels on the floor and squeezing them out into a bucket. His bucket needed to be dumped. He picked it up and walked to the top of the stairs.

Anastasia was splayed out on all fours about half-way up. She straightened quickly.

"Hi, Henry," she said. "I was just coming up."

"Oh," Henry said. At the sound of her sister's voice, Henrietta came scurrying out of Henry's room.

"Anastasia, you're awful!" Henrietta said. "You were eavesdropping!"

"No, I wasn't." Her eyes went big. "I was just coming to ask you something. Can I come up?"

"No," Henrietta said. "You were sneaking."

"It's okay," Henry said. "You can come up." He put the bucket down and moved aside. Anastasia climbed the remaining stairs quickly, trying not to look at her sister. Henrietta was making faces.

Anastasia stepped into Henry's doorway. Henry and Henrietta stood behind her. "Where'd you get all the posters?" she asked. The wall was completely covered with images of a basketball player, arms crossed, glaring. The posters were all taped together into a single sheet. Most were vertical, some were leaning, and one was upside down. Another one dangled from the ceiling, where Henrietta had not yet finished her taping.

"Dad gave them to me for Henry's room," Henrietta said. "He had them in the barn."

"All the same one?" Anastasia asked.

"Yeah, I don't mind," Henry said. Anastasia looked down at the still-wet floor. "Were you trying to keep a fish?" she asked. "Mom wouldn't mind a fish."

"No," Henry said.

"Frogs?"

"Nope."

"Salamanders?"

"Uh-uh," Henry said.

"Then what's the water from?"

"Nothing," Henrietta said.

"A rain cloud," Henry answered.

Anastasia stepped into Henry's room. Henrietta followed, standing right beside her.

Anastasia felt the bed. Then she saw the worms.

"I wish you would tell me about your secret. I've been wanting to spy, but Penny won't let me. Why won't you tell? I won't tell on you. Penny and I can keep a secret."

"Penny can," Henrietta said. She crossed her arms and shook back her hair.

Anastasia looked hurt. "I keep secrets!"

"Who told Mom about the rat skulls in the barn?" Henrietta asked.

"Well, I didn't mean to."

"Who told Becky Taller about the fort in the chestnut trees?"

"I don't even like Becky Taller!"

"Well, who told her, then? Who told Dad about the boots we were getting him for his birthday?"

"He forgot! He was still surprised."

"Who told Mom when I tried to climb the water tower?"

"I did not tell that!"

"You climbed the water tower?" Henry asked. "The tall one on the other side of town?"

"Yeah. Dad came and got me before I could get very high because someone told." She stared at Anastasia.

"It wasn't me," Anastasia said. "It really wasn't. I promise."

"Well, you told all the other times."

"Not on purpose. If you tell about the water and the worms, then I promise I won't tell anyone, not even Penny."

"If we told you, we would tell Penny," Henrietta said.

"I already told you," Henry said. "It came from a rain cloud."

Anastasia looked at him and curled her lip. "That's not very nice. Most water probably came from a rain cloud."

"We might tell you soon," Henry said. "I have to go dump the bucket." He scooped the towels up, carried them to the bucket, and started down the stairs. Anastasia followed him down onto the landing.

"Henry?" she asked.

"Yeah?"

"Do you think I can't keep a secret?"

He stopped and looked at her. "I don't know, can you?"

"It's kind of hard, but sometimes I can."

"Okay. I'll tell you a secret. Don't tell anybody."

"Okay."

"I don't want to go back to Boston."

"Oh." She looked disappointed. "What about your parents?"

"I hope they're okay, but I don't want to go back. They would never let me have a knife or ride in the back of the truck or drink soda or play baseball without a helmet."

"Real baseball players wear helmets," Anastasia said.

"They made me take a special class when I wet the bed."

"You wet the bed?"

"I used to."

"I won't tell anybody."

"Okay," Henry said, and he went into the bathroom. Anastasia went downstairs. She didn't tell anyone. It would have been harder if Penelope had asked.

"I thought he was keeping a fish," she whispered to Penelope. "But Henrietta said they weren't."

That night, Henry read on the dry end of his bed until he was sure his aunt and uncle were asleep. Then he pulled down the sheet of posters and looked at his collection of doors. He got out the chisel Henrietta had brought him and began prying and scraping at the remaining plaster.

Downstairs, Frank told Dotty not to worry about the scratching noise, rolled over, and went back to sleep.

Henry worked much faster with a chisel, and he was getting the hang of how the old plaster broke off.

He was also still heavily caffeinated from the barbeque and not even slightly tired.

The plaster in the upper corners came off quickly, and he tipped his dresser onto his bed so he could stand on its side to reach the very top of the wall where the ceiling peaked. There were no little doors that high, just a wooden panel crowning the whole wall. He climbed down off his dresser, stood it back up on the floor, and tried to quietly pull his bed away from the wall to get at the bottom.

Henrietta came in just as he finished moving his bed. She had waited a very long time for her sisters to fall asleep.

Most of the plaster behind the bed came off quickly because water had seeped down behind it and loosened it up. But the bottom corners still took the two children a great deal of time to clear off. The plaster was thinner there, cracked easily, and came off in tiny pieces.

When Henry finished and stepped back to look at his wall, the caffeine was gone and he was tired enough to fall asleep standing up. His arms and wrists were sore, and yawns came with almost no break between them. Henrietta, who had been sweeping and cleaning while Henry chipped, stopped as well and stood beside him.

"How many are there?" she asked.

Henry yawned. "I don't know. A lot. They're pretty small."

Henrietta started counting. Henry was too tired to count, so he just waited for her to finish.

"Ninety-nine," she said finally. "There are ninety-nine. Ninety-nine is a lot."

"Yeah." Henry yawned again.

"Should we go dump all the plaster now?" Henrietta asked.

Henry yawned again. He nodded. He couldn't talk.

The blanket was not piled as high as it had been the last time, but it was still very heavy. An exhausted Henry heaved his makeshift sack, and Henrietta followed him, picking up the pieces that he dropped.

When they arrived outside, the night air roused them a bit, but not much. Every time Henry yawned, Henrietta's jaw quaked and then opened wide as she fought one of her own.

The two of them finally made it to the irrigation ditch, watched the plaster slide down into the oily-looking night water, and sat down.

"I fell asleep here last time," Henry said. "It was early, but the sun was up. Your dad found me. He didn't even ask what I was doing."

"He never does."

"I'd like to sleep here again. It's much nicer than inside."

"You'd get cold."

"It's not that cold out here," Henry said. "It's just nice."

"I've done it before," Henrietta said. "Eventually you still get cold. Have you ever slept outside at night?"

Henry shook his head.

"Not even in a tent?"

Henry shook his head again. "I slept in a sleeping bag once. Mom said I had to keep it on top of my bed, but I slept on the floor. She thought I'd fallen out of bed." He was staring at the moon's strange face. Henrietta didn't say anything. He turned to look at her. She was asleep in the grass. Her mouth was open.

"Henrietta," he said. He poked her in the shoulder, and she woke. "We should go inside, or we'll both fall asleep."

"Okay," she muttered, and he helped her up. The two of them dragged bare feet through the beautifully damp grass, a wet and dirty blanket dragging behind them.

Henry said goodbye to Henrietta at her door, climbed his stairs, and threw his blanket on his bed. Where it had been wet, it was now filthy with dust that would not shake off. He didn't care. He didn't even bother to reattach his sheet of posters. He dropped his clothes and climbed onto his bed, put his head in the corner, remembered something, reached over, turned off his light, and closed his eyes in the darkness.

Henry didn't know if he had been asleep for hours or if he had only just gotten into bed. All he knew was that there was a light on in his room. It was supposed to be dark. What does that matter? his sleeping mind wondered. He didn't open his eyes. His bare feet squirmed around on the wet part of his sheets.

Suddenly he was wide awake. The light was shining across the end of his bed, lighting his damp feet. It was coming from the post office box.

Henry sat up and slid to the end of his bed, kicking his tangled bedding to the floor. Holding his breath, he looked through the narrow glass panel. Inside the darkness of the box, a single postcard leaned against the left side. Beyond that, the box opened onto a yellow room glowing with light. Henry's mind, back up to normal speed, remembered the key in his pants pocket.

Henry jumped off his bed and rustled through the sheet-and-blanket pile on the floor, hunting for his pants. When he found them, he reached for the pocket, then he panicked. What if the key had fallen out when he fell down at first base? Or when he fell down at second base? Or in right field? Then his fingers found the string and pulled it out.

The key swung and spun in the dim light. Henry hopped back onto his bed and felt for the keyhole. He pressed the key to the lock. Nope. He flipped the key around and tried again. It slid into place. He turned it, felt the latch release, and pulled open the little door.

Henry was peering through a mailbox into somewhere else. The somewhere else was mostly yellow. Then Henry heard someone whistling, and a pant leg came into view not two feet from Henry's face.

CHAPTER SEVEN

The pant leg was gray. It shifted, shuffled, and then stood still. The whistling slowed and stopped. A thick hand, wiry with black hair, reached down and slid a long envelope into Henry's box, next to the old post-card. Then the pant leg moved on, just one step judging from the click of the shoes, but out of Henry's range of vision.

Henry did not wonder if he was dreaming. He was too surprised for that. Instead, he stared, hardly breathing, into the yellow place. He could still hear the whistling, sometimes faint and distant, sometimes closer. He could hear the clicking of shoes as the pant legs walked about, but he only saw them walk by once more. The yellow place was not something that would have normally intrigued Henry, and a man's pant leg never would have. But seeing them just through a small box in his bedroom wall, which he knew to be an exterior wall facing the barn and miles of fields, made them far more interesting. And so Henry stared for quite a long time, at nothing much, which should never have been there.

When a boy finds a spider that isn't moving, he generally stops to examine it. If it persists in its lack of motion, even if it looks like it might be dangerous, he will poke it with a stick, just to see what it does. If it's a snake, he might use a longer stick or even a well-tossed rock. Henry was in a similar situation. He was looking at something more surprising than most people imagine possible. And yet it wasn't doing much.

Henry didn't have a stick. He didn't have a rock. So he reached up and pushed the long envelope back through the box and heard it drop to the floor on the other side. The whistling stopped. The yellow place was silent for a moment, and then the shoes began clicking toward him. Half a pant leg came into view. The leg inside it bent. A hand passed by. It traveled to the floor, then passed back the other way. It was holding the envelope.

"Hmm," a voice said. Henry caught his breath as a face, cocked sideways, came into view and looked straight at him. It was a man's face, long and thin, with a biggish gray mustache. The man peered inside the box while the hand came up and reslotted the envelope. Then the man stood, the whistling began once more, and the feet clicked their way elsewhere. Henry began breathing again.

It did not take Henry very long to become uncomfortable, hunched over with his face filling the small door. He tried shifting his weight, sitting instead of kneeling, but his neck kept kinking and his back ached. Finally, he pushed the sheet of posters to the far end of the room and slid off the bed onto the floor. He sat facing the cupboards, with his back against the opposite wall and his feet under his bed. From this position, he stared at the little rectangle of yellow light. But he didn't stare for long, because now that he was finally comfortable, he fell asleep.

When he woke, his right cheek was resting on his shoulder, his neck was kinked, and the light was gone. Henry hit his shin on the bottom of his bed standing up, yelped, then crawled onto his bed and felt for the small door. When he found it, he pulled out the long envelope and the postcard and dropped them on his bed. Then he sat and stared at the darkness, wondering what he should do next. He put his hand in the small post office box and felt around. Then he reached in deeper. It was only about a foot deep, and his hand quickly found the open back. He had an idea. With his left hand, he felt around for the latch on the door to the wind and trees. It slid easily, and the door swung open, letting in its earthy smell. That door was just above the little mailbox; a two-inch strip of wood was all that separated them.

Leaving his right hand in the mailbox, Henry leaned to the side and put his left hand in the bigger cupboard. He waddled as close to the wall as he could get, until he thought both of his arms had to be sticking out the other side of the cupboards. Then, resting his chin on the wall, he felt for his hands. His right hand waggled around in the air, touching nothing. His left squished against something soft and damp. His hands were in two very different places, but his mind knew that they ought to be touching just on the other side of the wall. Adjusting to push farther into the mailbox, he bent his arm and reached as high as he could. His fingers twiddled around and felt an envelope. He had found the back of another post office box. He reached to the side and found another one.

Henry pulled his arms back through and rubbed his hands together. The back of the mailbox was apparently in a wall in a post office somewhere. The front was in his bedroom. The back of the other cupboard was in a forest or somewhere with trees. The front was in his bedroom. His left hand had felt moss and dirt in some place where it had just rained. His right had been in a post office, fingering other people's mail. His body was in his bedroom.

Henry sat in the dark for a long time, thinking thoughts that led nowhere and asking questions he couldn't answer. Eventually, breathing in the air that crawled through his wall from some other place, he slept again. He slept with both little doors open. And while he slept, he dreamed.

Henry stood barefoot in a green place. His toes curled and uncurled, digging into wet, thick moss. And there were trees. Enormous trees. It was a forest, but the trees were far apart, at least one hundred feet in most places. The canopy intermingled above him, sprawling out from the straight-trunked, smooth-skinned towers that had waited to throw out branches until they had reached well into the sky.

Henry was on a gentle slope, almost flat where he stood. But below him he could see the tops of trees. This and the coldness of the air told him he was on a mountain. Henry looked up the hill behind him, at the green, mossed earth and the trunks of great trees. He watched himself walk. He was not controlling his walk or his pace or what he looked at. He was simply following along as he wandered through the dream. He could feel the water squeeze out of the moss between his toes. He could smell the cold air and feel it in his lungs.

He wanted to stop and run his hands along the smooth bark of the trees, to grip a great wooden belly with his arms. Instead, he walked and soon found himself in a clearing surrounded only by grass and sky. The slope rose only a little farther, and there at the top, a great rectangular slab of stone lay flat. It was almost as tall as Henry, and its edges were rounded.

Henry watched his hand reach out. The stone had been smooth once. Now moss and time had roughed its skin. Henry left his hand on its surface as he walked all the way around. On the other side grew the last tree.

This tree was thicker than those on the mountain's slopes, and not as tall. Its lowest branches were as broad as most trees he had ever seen. It was an old tree and looked as if it was dying. At the base of the trunk gaped a wide crack. Inside, the floor was all earth and rot. The wind was stronger on the top of the mountain and poured constantly through the old branches and their leaves.

Then Henry saw the dog. It was black and very large. It rushed up to the ancient tree and tried to force its head into the crack, pawing and scratching. Then it leapt away and ran to the slab of stone and scraped at the earth along its base. When it stood again, it hesitated, flaring its nostrils. It looked at Henry, or at where Henry was standing. The dog was huge, like a mastiff or a Dane, and with two steps it stood directly in front of Henry, its head nearly as wide as his waist. It cocked its head and smelled. Then it crouched and ran back to the tree.

It didn't make sense. Henry felt that he belonged there on that hill, that he knew the dog. His sleeping mind groped and grasped at old memories and found nothing it could hold.

Then the dog turned to him and said in a soft, feminine voice, "I don't think we should tell him. It's not real news and won't accomplish anything tonight, anyhow."

The dream swirled. Henry couldn't see the tree, but the stone was still there.

"They're his parents. Why would I be keepin' secrets about his parents?" said another voice.

"It's not a secret. It's just not helpful," the dog said.

"I know more than he does, and I don't see how that's right."

"Well, you'll always know more than he does."

"What are you saying?"

"Frank, they're not even his parents. Are you going to tell him that, too?"

Henry opened his eyes. He was on his bed, in his bedroom's darkness. The voices were very low. He could just make them out.

"If you tell him, at least wait until morning. It

wouldn't do any good talking to him now." There was silence. Then Frank muttered something Henry couldn't hear.

"Do you smell something?" Dotty asked. "The air feels crisp."

"No," Frank said. "I don't. The air feels like air to me."

"Okay, then," Dotty answered. "Come back down to bed." Henry could hear footsteps and realized Frank had been just outside his doors. It sounded like Dotty was still standing on the stairs. The creaking began, and Henry knew they were both walking back down.

It was a strange thing for Henry to hear. But he was more immediately relieved that Uncle Frank hadn't come into his room. Henry sat up and shut the cupboard doors. Then he turned on his lamp and put the sheet of posters back on the wall. When he was done, he curled up at the top of his bed and turned off his light.

Some of his dream was disappearing, already losing itself in his mind, but he remembered the dog talking, and he remembered what it had said. He remembered waking and what his aunt and uncle had said.

His parents weren't really his parents.

Henry was almost relieved. He still hoped that they

would be all right. But he wouldn't mind if they didn't come back until he was old enough to go to college. As long as they were comfortable.

Henry woke up and rolled over. Someone was knocking on his door.

"Come in," he said.

Frank stepped in and sat down on the bed.

"Hi, Uncle Frank." Henry sat up and yawned, as nervous as he was tired. He tried not to look at his posters.

"Mornin', Henry." Frank wasn't looking at Henry. He was looking through the bedroom doors, down the attic, and out the window at the end. "I was gonna tell you somethin' last night, but Dots thought I should wait until mornin'. So here I am."

Henry waited. When Frank didn't say anything else, he tried to help things along. "What is it?" he asked.

"Oh, well, yesterday a man calls up real late. He's with the government, and he tells us that your parents are alive. Been a ransom demand or some such."

"Oh," Henry said. "Is that it?"

"Yeah. Your aunt Dots didn't think it was a big deal. She thought it was awful late for someone to call us up just to state the obvious. Personally, I was surprised. Wouldn't have shocked me a bit if they'd knocked Ursula over the head. Amazes me they've kept her alive this long." Frank rubbed his jaw. He hadn't shaved. "I guess there's money in it for 'em. How long's it been now? A month?"

"About. They told me a couple weeks before school was out."

"Hmm," Frank said, and he just sat there.

"Uncle Frank?" Henry asked.

"Yeah?"

"Are they really my parents?"

"Nope," Frank said, and kept staring out the window.

"Oh," Henry said.

"Did you wet the bed?" Frank asked.

"No." Henry blushed and swung his legs onto the floor.

"Strange," Frank said. "Feelin' a little damp in my seat."

"Yeah, there was a spill."

"Anyway . . ." Frank slapped his hands on his knees and stood up. "Thought you should know. Your aunt and I are heading into the city. Penny and Anastasia are comin' along. We should be back in time for a late dinner. I'm sure you got plenty to do. Ever use a computer? Got solitaire on mine, if you like. Don't tell the girls I let you."

"You're leaving us here by ourselves?"

"You and Henrietta," Frank said. "She wanted to stay. Said you would, too. Do you wanna come?"

"No. I'll be fine. But isn't that neglect? Can't you get into trouble?"

"Don't know why we would. Your aunt's already put sandwiches in the fridge for the two of you and left instructions for the casserole if we're late comin' back."

Frank stepped out of Henry's room and then glanced back, looking over the wall of posters.

"Don't get into too much trouble," he said, and headed for the stairs.

Henry tried to smile, then he lay back down. A few minutes later, he heard the truck erupt into life and the noise of spraying gravel as it pulled away.

Henry didn't feel like getting up, and so he didn't. It wasn't long before he heard Henrietta running up the stairs.

"Up, up, up!" Henrietta said, jumping on his bed. Her loose curls seemed to fill the room. "Everybody's gone."

"Go out," Henry said. "I have to get dressed."

She did, but she kept talking from the attic.

"Mom and Dad were going to take us, too, but I said I didn't want to and that I thought you wanted to go to Zeke's, so they left us. Now we can figure out the doors, and we won't even have to be quiet."

"I got the mailbox open last night."

"What?" Henrietta came back into the room while

Henry was trying to shove his head through the sleeve of his shirt. "What was in it?"

"Some mail. I haven't looked at it yet." He straightened his shirt out and pulled it on.

"Mail?" she asked. "Why would there be mail?" She picked up his rumpled blanket.

"It's a mailbox," Henry said.

Henrietta ignored him. "Where is it?"

"Henrietta," Henry said. "Last night was really weird."

She dropped his blanket and looked at him. The two of them sat on his bed, and he told her everything, about the yellow room and the man's face and pushing the envelope back so it fell and reaching his arms through the cupboards and not being able to touch on the other side. "This hand is still muddy," he finished, and held out his palm.

Henrietta was impressed. "You could see his face?"

"Yep."

"And he had a mustache?"

"Yep."

"And you could see through into a yellow room?"

"Yep."

"Could he see you?"

"I don't think so. He stared right at me but didn't seem to notice."

"And you weren't dreaming?"

"Nope. I dreamed later."

Henrietta whistled through her teeth, then reached out and touched the poster-covered wall of cupboards. "They're magic for sure. I didn't really think they would be. I wonder how we go through."

"Go through?"

"Yeah. The whole point of magic doors is to try and go through them to somewhere else."

"But they're too small."

"Where's the mail?" Henrietta said. "Let's read the mail. Do you need breakfast?"

"Yeah, okay. The mail was on the bed," Henry said. "It might have slid off."

Henrietta found the mail, and Henry put on his socks. Then the two of them headed down to the kitchen. Henrietta grabbed the milk while Henry picked his cereal. While Henry chewed, Henrietta examined the first piece of mail. It was the postcard. The picture was a black-and-white photo of a lake and a large boat. The boat was strange. People stood along a second-story deck, around three smokestacks. A huge paddle wheel was attached to one end. Unlike on the old American riverboats, the paddle was attached to the front beneath a swooping hull that looked like it belonged on a Viking ship.

Henrietta showed it to Henry, then turned it over. Everything was written in a tall and narrow cursive. She read slowly.

Sola 16
Simon,
  The children are both ill, and the wind nips a bit at my thin bones. I shall give you electric catfish next time you visit. Come soon.
          Love from Lake Tinsil,
          Gerty

The two of them looked at each other.

"Wow," Henrietta said.

"What does it mean?" Henry asked.

"I don't know. It's a letter. Grandpa's, probably. His name was Simon." Henrietta squinted. "The picture looks old."

"It says something else on the bottom, only it's printed." Henry leaned over his cousin. " 'The proud *Valkr* in her mother waters.' Is that the boat? The *Valkr*?"

"Must be," Henrietta said. "Which one do you want to do next?"

Two envelopes rested on the table in front of

Henrietta. Henry recognized the long one he had pushed into the mailroom. The other was nearly square.

"But there were only two," he said.

"I know that," Henrietta said. "Which one do you want to read first?"

"No," Henry said. "There was only the postcard and the long envelope." He reached over and took both. "Where did you get this one?" he said, holding up the square envelope.

Henrietta shrugged. "With the other ones. They were all between your mattress and the wall."

The square envelope was milk white and sealed with a glob of what looked like green wax. The long envelope was cream-colored and had handwriting on the back. The writing was tight and slanted, almost like calligraphy. Henry read it out loud, but slowly. " 'To the Master of the Seventy-seventh Box, Seventh Row of Lionesse, DX of Byzanthamum.' I don't think that's a proper address. What's the address here?"

"Eleven Grange Road," Henrietta said. "It got delivered. Just open it."

Henry slid his finger under the flap. The paper tore easily, and he pulled out a stiff folded sheet. The handwriting inside was the same. He squinted at it and began reading.

Midsummer
Sir,

In the course of our contempora ritualisms, we have discerned that certane of the lost byways have been both aired et stirred. We need not explain the means of our discernimentata, as you must be no strange face to our scientistics et were no doubt awarned that you had notified us of your presence as ripely as you had done so.

Former or freshe, master of the box you are. You fanger-grase the compassi, et you must kendle our intentions. Wake the old daughter of the second sire. We will not live for less. Do this et feel your freedoms breathe. Fail, et our order will sophistri in strength. See, the blud-eagle is no hen.

> Darius,
> First amung the Lastborn Magi,
> W.D. of Byzanthamum

Henry put the letter down and looked at Henrietta.

"I don't think you read that right," she said. "Give it to me."

Henry slid her the letter and dribbled soggy cereal off his spoon while he watched her read.

"This doesn't make sense," Henrietta said. "Whoever wrote it must have been nuts."

"You don't think it's about us?" Henry asked. "I could be the master of the box. It's in my room."

Henrietta raised her eyebrows and looked at him.

"What?" Henry asked.

"It's in our house," she said.

"Yeah . . . ?"

"You're not the master of anything, Henry." She looked down at the letter. "And it wouldn't matter if you were. This is total gibberish. Whoever the master of the box is, he's supposed to wake up the daughter of a second sire. A sire is a king, right? Do you know any kings, Henry?"

"Maybe," Henry said, stirring his cereal. "You wouldn't know."

Henrietta laughed. "Right. I'm going to open the other one." She picked up the square envelope and turned it over so the seal was up. The green glob shone in the light like glass. It had been stamped with a signet, and a thick lip bulged up around the image of a man's head. He was bearded, and his eyes were blank, pupil-less. Leaves grew in his beard and out of his nose and mouth. Vines crawled from his ears and were wrapped around his forehead like a crown.

"That's a little creepy," Henrietta said. She tried to slide her finger along the paper to pop the seal off, but it wouldn't budge. She tried to tear the paper but couldn't so much as wrinkle it. She dropped the envelope on the table and stood up. "I'm getting scissors," she said.

Henry shifted in his seat. "Don't bother," he said. "They won't work." He looked up at her. "It's just like Grandfather's door. You won't be able to get it open."

He took the envelope in his hands and ran his fingers over the paper.

"I'm still getting scissors." Henrietta turned away. She didn't take a step. A pop like the sound of a knuckle cracking had come from behind her.

She turned around. "What was that?" she asked.

"Um . . . ," Henry said. "I touched the seal."

"What?"

"The seal. On the letter. I touched it." Henry pointed toward the table.

The seal had divided through the green man's forehead, around his nose, and down through his beard.

"It's broken," Henrietta said. "Split right in half." She picked up the envelope and tried to open it. The paper wouldn't move.

"I think it's for me," Henry said.

Henrietta looked at him, looked at the seal, and then handed him the envelope.

It was all one piece of thick paper, not an envelope at all, and it unfolded easily in Henry's hands.

He held the paper out. "Do you want to see, too?" he asked.

"Read it out loud," Henrietta said, dropping back into a chair. Her hand snuck up to her mouth, and she began chewing on her thumbnail.

Henry looked over the paper, more than a little surprised at what he saw. The writing wasn't writing at all; it had been typed. And typed on what looked to be a very old typewriter. Every *T* and *K* stuck out high. It was much easier to read than the other letter.

Issuance from the Central Committee of
    Faeren for the Prevention of Mishap
(District R.R.K.)

Composed and Adopted under Emergency
    Guidelines
(*Book of Faeren,* VI.iii)
Delivered via the Island Hill of Badon
    Chapter
(District A.P.)

To Whom We May Concern:
    Testimony has been presented in the
Hill of the Faeren (District R.R.K.)
regarding certain gates that were once
created without authority and were

frivolously exploited to the great detriment of five of our most ancient districts and two civilizations. Said gates were believed to have been destroyed, and/or/perhaps severed or sealed.

Said testimony in said hill of aforementioned district established the following:

(a) That gates had either not been destroyed, nor severed nor sealed, or that gates had been destroyed or severed or sealed but have been rebuilt, repaired, or opened; (b) That beside said gates sleeps a male child, timid in all habit, who both snoreth and whimpereth in his slumber (henceforth: Whimpering Child); (c) That Whimpering Child is reprehensible and a shame to all who pursue wisdom or have earned gray hairs or fleshy scars, struggling to prevent mishap in the service of this district, past, present, and fut.

Having found the testimony sound,

the Central Committee of Faeren for
the Prevention of Mishap (District
R.R.K.) issues the following
notification, to be delivered by
members of the Island Hill of Badon
Chapter (District A.P.), who provided
above testimony:

That if Whimpering Child through
ignorant or malicious meddling shall
unearth, unbind, or release evils long-
defeated or evils young and undefeated,
he shall be deemed fully responsible
by the CCFPM of this district and be
destroyed forthwith.

Let Whimpering Child beware.

When the seal has been broken,
notice shall be considered given.

Notice has been given.

>Ralph Radulf
>
>Chair CCFPM
>
>>(District R.R.K.)
>
>C and A under EG
>
>(per *B.F.* VI.iii)

Henry looked up at his cousin. "Someone knows I found the cupboards."

"You don't know that," Henrietta said. "It doesn't

have to be about you." She forced a smile. "You do whimper, though."

"I don't think it's funny," Henry said. "Somebody's been watching me. That's freaky."

Henrietta shrugged, but she slipped her thumbnail back between her teeth.

Henry ate his cereal, and the two hurried back upstairs. They tore down the poster wallpaper and stood by his bed staring at the doors.

The doors stared back.

"I want to look in the little mailbox first," Henrietta said. "But then I think we should just bang on them and see if they're stuck, like the first one was."

Henry gave Henrietta the key to the mailbox. She pushed her hair out of her face and hunkered down so she could unlock the box and look through the little black space. Henry stood on his bed and used the butt end of the chisel to rap on all the metal latches and slides.

"Are you sure it was yellow in here?" Henrietta asked.

"Yes. But I think it might be in a different time zone. That's why it's dark now."

Henrietta sat up. "I'm going to come watch with you tonight. I hope Anastasia and Penelope sleep hard. Have you tried all the ones near the floor? I want to see those. Let's pull the bed back."

Henry got off the bed, and the two of them pulled it as far away from the wall as they could, which was only about a foot and a half. Henrietta pulled a rubber band out of her pocket and began twisting her hair back into a ponytail. "I like that one by the floor," she said. "The black one." The door was about nine inches square and extremely dark. The dust from the plaster stood out against it like chalk on a blackboard.

"Are you sure? You don't think it looks sad?"

"No. It looks magic."

"But it's black."

Henrietta smiled. "That's why it looks magic. It's more ebony, anyway. That's a nicer black."

Henry looked at the black cupboard more closely. For some reason, he had avoided looking at it before. Of course, it had been late and he had been tired when he first chipped the plaster off it, but he hadn't really liked it then, moving on quickly and not looking back. He didn't know why.

"Did you try it?" Henrietta asked.

Now that she'd asked, Henry knew he hadn't.

"I don't remember," he said.

Henrietta looked at him. "Well, try it now."

Henry didn't want to. In the center of the door was a very small metal knob. He reached down and felt it. It was cold. He tried to turn it.

"It won't turn," he said, and stood back up.

"Is it supposed to?" Henrietta asked. She squeezed past Henry, draped herself over the bed, gripped the small knob, and pulled. The door came off in her hand. A gold chain attached to the back rattled out behind the door.

Henrietta looked surprised. "I got it open," she said.

Henry desperately wanted to leave the room. "I don't think it's a good door at all," he whispered. A lump was forming in his gut. "I think I'm going to be sick."

Henrietta wasn't listening. With her other hand, she pulled on the chain.

"It's attached inside the cupboard," she said. "The whole thing just comes off and sticks back on. Oh, look at this." She slid farther off the bed and reached into the dark opening.

Henry threw up on the floor beside the cupboards. Then he passed out.

When he came to, he felt much better. Henrietta was sitting on the bed looking down at him.

"Are you okay?" she asked. "You threw up on the floor. I dropped an old towel over it. You can clean it up later."

"I don't like that cupboard," Henry said. He was between his bed and the cupboard wall. He didn't try to sit up. "It made me sick. Did I pass out?"

"Yeah. You were still breathing, so I wasn't worried. Anastasia used to hold her breath until she passed out all the time."

"Did you close the cupboard?"

"Yes. I don't think it was the cupboard, though. I still like it. Look what was inside." She held up a key. It was much bigger than the last one, and older, too, a skeleton key. "I think it might be the key to Grandfather's bedroom. Dad has other keys like it, and they look like this. I waited for you to wake up to try it."

Henry propped himself up. A ratty green towel sat in a lump at his feet. "But why would Grandfather's key be in there?" he asked. "The doors were plastered way too long ago. You'd remember if it had only been two years."

"Could be more than one key. Plus, they're magic cupboards. If you can see a mailman's face in your wall, then I don't think a key is that big a deal."

"I don't think a key will work. I think something is keeping it shut."

"Well, let's try." Henrietta stood up. Henry stood up after her, wondering if he would be sick again. He looked back at the towel.

"It's just a little puke and the towel kind of hides the smell," Henrietta said. "Come on."

The two of them pushed the bed out of the way, then walked down the attic stairs and around the landing. They stepped over the hole in the floor and the tangled and shredded carpet and stood before the old and now-defaced door.

"You do it," Henrietta said, and held out the key.

"You found it," Henry said.

"Yeah, but I want you to do it."

"Why?"

"I don't know," she said. "I think you should."

Henry took the key and found the hole in the wood, which had once been protected by a brass cover plate. He stuck the key in and twisted. It caught on something, and then clicked. He stepped back.

"There's not a knob," he said.

"Push it."

Henry reached out and touched the mulched surface of the door. He pushed. The door swung wide open without a sound.

"Oh my goodness," Henrietta said. The two of them peered in.

The large bed was made. A clock on the nightstand ticked beside an open book, face down to save someone's place. Behind that was a clear glass vase, with fresh flowers. One of the windows was open, and the curtain ghosted in the breeze.

"Are they fake?" Henrietta asked.

"What?"

She pointed. "The flowers. In the vase by the bed."

"Doesn't look like it. There's water in the vase." Henry stepped forward.

"Don't go in, Henry," Henrietta said.

"Why?"

"There shouldn't be flowers. Grandfather died two years ago, and the door's been locked the whole time. There shouldn't be flowers. And look, the window's open. The window isn't supposed to be open. It's always shut from the outside."

Henry looked around the room. "The flowers have some brown spots."

"But they're not dry. And where's the dust?" Henrietta leaned into the doorway, nervously pulling at her ponytail. "Grandfather?" she asked. "Are you there?" She stepped back on the landing.

"I think we should go in," Henry said.

Henrietta didn't answer. Henry stepped across the threshold. He looked around.

"Anything?" Henrietta asked.

"He's not here," Henry said. "Just lots of books."

"Look behind the door," Henrietta said. She was biting a nail.

Henry did and found a purple robe hanging on a peg. He stood very still, staring at it.

"What?" Henrietta asked. "What's back there?"

"I've seen . . . ," Henry began, but a wall went up in his mind. The robe was just purple. And dirty, and long. Irritated, Henry reached out and clenched the fabric in a fist. He threw himself against the block in his mind.

Henrietta stepped into the room and looked at him. Her face was worried.

"Henry?" she asked. "Are you okay?"

Henry let go of the robe. He licked his lips. "Was Grandfather short?" he asked. "I had a dream—maybe—where someone was wearing this purple thing. A short old man. Coming out of the bathroom."

Henrietta stared at him. "Grandfather was tall. Really tall. You saw someone in the bathroom?"

"I don't know," Henry said. "Maybe not. But I've got a picture of him in my head. I don't know why."

Henrietta walked to the bed, looked out the window, crossed her arms, and shivered. "This is weirding me out, Henry."

Henry picked up the book on the nightstand and turned it over. "It's a journal."

Henrietta looked at him. "Grandfather's journal?"

"It's full. It looks like he was just reading it."

"I don't think he was. Dad says he was reading him a book about an old war when he died. Somebody else must be reading it."

"Who?" Henry asked.

She looked right at Henry, her eyes wide. "Who'd you see in the bathroom? I don't know." She shivered again and rubbed her arms.

Henry looked back at the purple robe on the door and then down at the journal. He began reading.

"Henrietta," he said. "This is about the cupboards."

"What?" She looked over his shoulder. The page on the right was covered with a drawing. The ink was blotchy, but there was no doubt what it was. It was Henry's cupboard wall. There was an outline for every cupboard door, and in the middle of all but one was a number. The page on the left had two columns of numbers, 1 to 98.

CHAPTER EIGHT

"Why are there only ninety-eight?" she said. "I thought we counted ninety-nine."

Henry cocked his head and scrunched his lips. "I think the door with the compass locks doesn't have a number."

Henrietta leaned closer. "What does it say by the numbers? Does it tell you how to get through?"

"I don't think so," Henry said.

"But what does it say?"

"About which one? There's ninety-eight of them."

"How about the mailbox?"

Henry looked around the diagram and found a little rectangle about where he thought the mailbox was. It had the number 77 written on it. He looked over to the other page and found 77. Beside the number were three words with slashes between them.

" 'Post/Byzanthamum/When?' " Henry read.

"I don't know what that means," Henrietta said. "Do you?"

" 'Post' means mail. Byzanthamum is a place. It was in one of the letters." He looked up at her. "I left the letters on my bed."

"I'll get them," Henrietta said. Henry could hear her running up the attic stairs while he looked over Grandfather's diagram.

She was breathing loudly when she stepped back into the room with the letters in her hand. "The crazy handwritten letter is addressed to the master of the seventy-seventh box," she said. "Read what it says for the black cupboard."

Instead, Henry looked at the one above the mailbox, the door that had rained on his bed. Its number was 56. Beside the 56 on the other page were the words "Commonwealth/Badon Hill/Same." Henry put out his hand, and Henrietta gave him the two letters. The top of the typed one said it had been delivered by the "Island Hill of Badon Chapter." He shivered. Someone must have dropped the letter onto his bed from the other side while he was sleeping.

"What's the black cupboard?" Henrietta asked. Henry found it on the bottom row. Or he thought he did. He couldn't be quite sure how many in from the end it was. Then he looked back at the list of numbers and found number 8.

" 'Endor,' " he said. "That's all it says, and it doesn't sound nice at all."

"It doesn't have to sound nice," Henrietta said. "Just exciting. What do you think it means?"

"I think it's a place. Badon Hill is a place. It's where the worms came from and the rain and the second letter. Endor's a place. They're all places on the other side of the cupboards."

"Do you think we can get through?"

"No."

"Why not?"

"We're too big."

Henrietta thought about this for a moment. "There has to be a way we can shrink."

"I don't think so."

"What about the other cupboard?" Henrietta asked. "What did it say again?"

"It says 'Post/Byzanthamum/When?'."

"The 'Byzanthamum' part sounds like a flower," she said. "It would be nice if it was a flower place."

"It's a post office."

"But what about outside the post office? If you went to the post office, you could go outside, and then where would you be?"

Henry had not thought of this. His mind had grasped, as far as it could grasp such a thing, that the cupboards in his room led to different places. But he had thought of those places like anyone else would think of a secret room in a house. He had only gotten as far as thinking of Badon Hill as a place with trees and Byzanthamum as a yellow post office. It had not even crossed his mind that these places could in turn lead to other places, which might lead to other places and to other places, as many places as there were stars or people or breaths in the wind.

"Do you think these might be whole different worlds?" he asked.

Henrietta didn't blink at the question. "I thought about that," she said. "Some of them might be, but I don't think so."

"Why not?"

"They just seem very here."

"Oh," Henry said.

Henrietta was reading over his shoulder. "Look," she said, and pointed. "This one says 'Arizona.' I've been to Arizona, and it's not in a different world."

Henry looked. She was right. "Arizona" was written beside the number 17.

"Which one is it?" Henry asked, and they both scanned the diagram for the number 17. They found it four up from the bottom on the left side. Then they read through the list for any other names they recognized. The rest of the words meant very little to them. "Aksum" reminded Henry of something, but he didn't know what.

When they'd read through the list, Henry closed the journal and sat on his grandfather's bed.

"What's wrong?" Henrietta asked. She sat beside him and took the book out of his hands. She turned it to the first page.

Henry sighed. "I don't think we should be doing this."

"You sound like Penelope," Henrietta said.

"Listen to me," Henry said. "Somebody, probably Grandfather, hid these cupboards. I don't think they're very nice. Especially not the black one. We should either tell your dad everything and let him figure out the cupboards or just leave the key to the room somewhere where he can find it."

"You're scared," Henrietta said. She wasn't looking at him.

"So? We've gotten two letters so far, and neither of them was very nice."

"Whimpering Child?" said Henrietta. "Don't worry. It's not that bad. It's normal for little kids to be scared."

Henry glared at her. "I'm older and bigger than you are."

Henrietta laughed and put her chin in the air. "I'm not scared."

"Oh, come on!" Henry snorted. "You were scared to come in this room."

"That's different," she said. "And I still didn't chicken out. I came in, and *I* even think somebody's been living in here." Henry didn't say anything, so she kept going. "I'm sure you can be as brave as a girl who is younger and smaller than you are if you try. Let's just find out a little more about the cupboards, and then we'll decide whether or not to tell Dad. Okay?" She grinned at him.

"Fine," Henry said. He couldn't have said anything else.

Henrietta looked down at the bed and around the room. "But let's not stay in here," she said. "Let's go up to your room."

Henry grabbed the letters, and the two of them stood up and walked to the door. Henrietta was carrying the journal.

Henry took the key out of the door and put it in his pocket. He pulled the edge of the door, let it swing as close to the jamb as it would go, then stuck his finger in the hole where the knob would have been and shut the door the rest of the way.

"Lock it, so it doesn't swing open," Henrietta said. Henry pushed on the door. It didn't move.

"It's already locked," he said, and the two of them, trying not to glance back, ran up the stairs to Henry's room and flopped onto his still-damp bed.

For a long time, they matched numbers and names to the cupboards on Henry's wall. When they started to lose track, Henrietta wrote the name and number of each cupboard on little pieces of paper that she cut out from one of her old school notebooks. Then she taped them to the doors, always careful to avoid stepping in Henry's little accident. When they were about halfway done, she bounced back onto Henry's bed and announced that she was tired of taping.

"I can tape for a bit," Henry said.

"No," Henrietta said. "That's not what I meant. I meant I want to be done looking at the cupboards now. I want to go through one."

"Well, we can't."

"I'm sure there's a way. Why else would Grandfather keep all of them?"

"He plastered them shut."

Henrietta wasn't listening. "I wish we could see through the dark one. You could reach through, though."

"Yeah." Henry was flipping through the pages of the journal. Most of it looked disappointing—just a bunch of stuff neither of them understood about wood grains and wind, and lots and lots of drawings and descriptions of the house. Beyond the two pages dedicated to the cupboards, they had found nothing helpful.

"I'm gonna reach through," she said, and sat up.

Henry tried to ignore her. He knew she would go straight to the black door, so he just kept turning pages and staring blankly at the old handwriting. She

surprised him by going to the Badon Hill door first.
She didn't ask for help with the stiff latch, and eventually it slid beneath her weight. The door opened, and
even though he wasn't looking, Henry smelled the
pleasant change in the room. Henrietta did, too.

"I wish my bedroom could smell like that," she
said, and breathed deeply with her face in the door.
Then she poked her hand through and began feeling
around.

Henry knew that she was feeling the same things he
had—soft, almost-damp earth and moss.

She held quite still for a moment before she pulled
her hand back. She smiled at Henry. "I could feel the
sun," she said, and turned back to the cupboard. "I
think I know how we could see through."

"How?" Henry said. He was looking now.

"It's not dark on the other side," Henrietta said.
"For some reason, the light just doesn't come through.
I think we need a periscope."

Henry laughed. "A periscope?" he asked. "Where
are we going to get one?"

"I have one in the barn. Mom and Dad gave it to
me for my last birthday. Dad made it. I'll be right
back."

She left Henry by himself sitting on the bed. He
was looking at the door to Badon Hill. Soon he was
feeling around the inside again. He pulled some

crumbling wood and a beetle back through and then reached again, as far as he could. There was no top, just rough, rotting sides and an earthy bottom. Suddenly he felt the sunlight on the back of his hand and fingers. He sat back and thought. A periscope might work. Henry looked down at the black door. If it did work, then Henrietta would want to look through that one, and he would be sick again. The green towel still marked the spot of his first embarrassment.

He pushed the towel with his toe. Then he bent over, rubbed the floor with it, stood up, and hurried downstairs, breathing through his mouth. In the kitchen, he rinsed the towel off in the sink, then climbed back up to the attic with fistfuls of paper towels. When he finished cleaning up, at least by a boy's standards, he went down to the second-floor bathroom and plugged the toilet trying to flush everything at once. He watched the toilet burble and stew until he heard Henrietta come up. He looked at the toilet again, mentally shrugged, and went back to his stairs.

When he reached his doorway, Henrietta was already trying to wiggle her periscope through the door to Badon Hill. She was having some trouble, but it finally slid through, pointing up at a very slight angle. She laughed out loud and clapped her hands.

"Turn the light off, Henry. I want to see if there's anything shining through before I look." Henry slid between the wall and the bed and over to the lamp, but he didn't turn it off.

"Which way is it pointing?" he asked.

"What do you mean?"

"I mean is your periscope looking up at the sky, down at the ground, or sideways? It won't look straight out."

Henrietta looked at him blankly. "Why not?"

"I think it must be pointing down."

Henry was right. Frank had made the periscope out of PVC pipe and old motorcycle mirrors. A viewing box was attached to the bottom, and Henrietta had it pointing up so she could look down into it. The length of pipe ran into the cupboard, and on the other end, where Henry and Henrietta couldn't see, was a box pointing the opposite direction from the first one—almost straight down at the ground.

Henrietta bent over the view box and looked.

"I can see!" she said. "It's all green."

"It's probably grass," Henry said.

Henrietta sat back up. "So how do we look out?" she asked.

"Well," Henry said, "we'll probably have to take the box off the other end."

"You mean break it?"

"No, I mean take it off, so we can look straight out. We can always put it back on."

Henrietta wriggled the pipe back through the cup-board and handed it to Henry. "Be careful. I don't want Dad to think I broke it."

"He wouldn't notice anyway." Henry gripped the pipe and pulled at the box on the top. He tugged and twisted until it came off in his hand.

"He didn't glue it," Henry said. "It will go back on easy."

This time Henry tried to shove the pipe through the cupboard, but he just fumbled with it. Finally, Henrietta took it and fed it through.

"Now turn off the light," she said. Henry did, and then he shut his two doors. He and Henrietta both caught their breath. A solid beam of sunlight shone up through the view box, through the wandering dust in the air, eventually arriving in a bright spot on Henry's ceiling.

"There's light," Henrietta managed.

"Look through," Henry said. Henrietta leaned slowly over the view box, blinked a bit, and then looked. After a moment, she pulled away from the box. Her eyes were watering.

"What did you see?" Henry asked.

"Some grass and tall trees and the sky, and then I looked right at the sun by accident. And a big rock. Let's put the box on. I want to look at the sides."

"Let me look first."

What Henry saw was green and upside down. He saw tall grass, blowing gently, around the end of the pipe. Beyond that was the gray, moss-topped surface of what seemed to be a large stone. Even farther were the tops of some very tall trees. Henry pushed his end of the periscope down as far as it would go, and the view climbed higher. There were leaves on the tops of trees but mostly a very blue sky, and in that blue sky was a single cloud.

He lifted the view box and tried to make out the stone. It was not long before he recognized it. And it was after he recognized it that he saw what looked like bones perched against the left end of the stone. A skull, almost nose up, was leaning against the gray wall of the rock. Moss flecked yellow and ivory spread beneath it. Henry couldn't see it well, but he could make out the long snout, part of an eye socket, and one row of upper teeth with big canines. His first thought was Wolf, then Dog, and finally Black Dog. Henry sat up quickly.

He had forgotten most of his dream, but the thought of the black dog brought it all pouring back. All the images of his climb, the trees, and the stone scurried through his mind.

"We're in the crack of the old tree," he said.

"What?" Henrietta said. "What do you mean?"

"I dreamed this place," Henry said. And he described it all for her, from the beginning to the end.

"We're looking out from the crack of the old tree where the big black dog was scratching."

Henrietta sat still for a moment, silent. Henry sat still, wondering what to think.

"Let's look in Endor," Henrietta said.

"What?"

"The black door. Let's look through that one now."

Henry shook his head. "I don't want to. I'll be sick again."

"No, you won't," Henrietta said. "You didn't dream anything bad about that door, did you? Oh, we should clean up where you threw up. I don't want to slip on the towel in the dark."

"I already did," Henry said. "When you were in the barn. But I plugged the toilet with the paper towels."

"Did it overflow?"

"Not while I was in there."

Henrietta laughed. "You just left it?"

"Yeah."

"There's a plunger right beside the toilet. Let's look through the black door."

"I don't want to."

"Well, then go sit out in the attic and I'll look." Henrietta slid toward the wall. "Or go down and plunge the toilet. You're being worse than Penny. She's never curious."

Henry stood up. He didn't say anything. Everything

he wanted to say would sound childish. He knew he was afraid of the black door, and he thought that he should be. But he was embarrassed that he had thrown up, and Henrietta made him feel stupid. So he opened his bedroom doors, stepped out with only a slightly offended grunt, and went to plunge the toilet. He shut the doors behind him, hoping that Henrietta might feel a little afraid in the dark.

Henry had never used a plunger before. Of course, there wasn't much that he *had* used before. He had read about various devices and implements in boring books that his father had given him for birthdays and Christmas, so he knew about the float mechanism in the toilet tank, about water filtration and anti-lock brakes. He had read nothing about plungers.

The plunger he was using was confusing him. The rubber part was black and somehow kept turning inside out. But Henry wasn't thinking too much about it, and when, after he had slopped it around the toilet bowl a bit, he reached over and flushed the toilet, he hardly noticed how close to overflowing the water came.

He was irritated with Henrietta and with himself. Why did he have to throw up just because he was scared? And pass out? And he was angry with Henrietta because she was being stupid. The door was obviously not a good door. More than that, he was angry with himself for leaving her alone to look through a door he was sure was bad. He shouldn't have let her. He was bigger than she was.

Suddenly all the water in the toilet gurgled and slurped its way down. Henry glanced at the toilet, wondered where all the water had gone, then flushed it again. Without watching to see what would happen, he stuck the plunger back onto its holder beside the toilet and headed upstairs.

He was preoccupied, collecting the words he would use to explain things to Henrietta, when his hand touched one of his doors. It was cold. He pulled the doors open quickly and stepped forward into the dark room. His bed was in the way.

"Henrietta," he said. Cold in the room sucked at him. His skin tightened and sent up bumps. His stomach knotted and burbled into his throat while his legs tried to collapse. He jumped onto the bed and lunged for his lamp. He knocked it over, but still found the small switch and pushed it.

Henrietta was lying on her face between the bed and the wall. Her left arm was up to the shoulder in the black cupboard.

Ignoring the pit of nausea in his stomach, Henry jumped to the floor, grabbed her shoulders, and tried to pull her away from the wall. She wouldn't budge.

On all fours above Henrietta, he leaned down and

reached into the cupboard. He swallowed a gag and moved his hand along the chilled skin of her arm. He knew when his hand had passed out of the cupboard because Henrietta's arm went from cold to frozen.

His fingers crawled down her arm until they felt a hand gripping her wrist, clenched tight. In a split second, the hand let go of Henrietta and grabbed Henry.

Henry yelled, tried to jump, and bent his elbow in the wrong direction in the cupboard. He twisted his hand hard, and pulled back. He was jerked against the wall, his head slamming against the knob of another cupboard. Loud words he did not understand poured out of the cupboard's mouth, and the cold grew stronger. Henry writhed, lungs full but not exhaling, teeth grinding, body flopping and pulling. Even while he fought, he felt sickness growing inside him, welling into his chest. He felt the fingers on his wrist slip and quickly reclamp farther up, around his forearm and his shirtsleeve. He put both knees up on the wall and pulled back. His sleeve, gripped tight, slid down around his wrist.

Henry didn't think about what he did. He had done it before on the playground. He had been made fun of then. He slithered his hand back inside his sleeve. The other hand gripped and regripped, but Henry was shedding his shirt quickly now. When his arm came free into the body of his shirt, he ducked his head down and pulled it out. The whole shirt disappeared into the cupboard, and he fell back onto the floor. Then, before he could pull her hand from the door, Henrietta's body slid closer to the wall. Henry turned, leaned across his bed, and grabbed his floppy-bladed knife off the nightstand.

This time, when he dropped to the floor beside Henrietta, he gripped Henrietta's shoulder with his right hand while his left, with thumb firmly holding the knife open, slid down her arm. When he thought he was almost to the back of the cupboard, he stopped and took a deep breath. Then he lunged straight through with the knife. The blade bit into something hard like bone but slipped and folded shut on his own fingers. On the other side of the cupboard, something shrieked. Henry felt Henrietta's arm go limp. He dropped the knife, yanked his hand back, and rolled Henrietta away from the wall. Then he grabbed the black door, shook the gold chain back in, and slapped the door in place. He kicked it tight and sat still with both of his feet against it, breathing heavily.

Henrietta wasn't stirring. Henry looked at his fingers. Three of them were leaking blood onto the floor. He shivered, noticing again how cold the room was, especially without his shirt. He wanted to check on

Henrietta. Instead, he sat for a very long time with his feet against the door to Endor. When enough time had passed that he was sure whoever it was couldn't get the door open from the other side, or wasn't going to try, he scooted over to Henrietta. She was almost snoring. He shook her a little.

"Henrietta," he said. She turned her head but didn't wake. "Henrietta," he said again, and shook her harder. He glanced up. Blake the cat was sitting on the bed looking at him. His white body was motionless, his ears were up, and his gray tail twitched. Henry stared back.

"Did you see that?" Henry asked. The cat looked at the black door, then jumped down to lick Henrietta's face with his sandpaper tongue. She opened her eyes and tried to sit up. Henry helped her.

"Are you okay?" he asked.

Henrietta yawned. "Where's your shirt?"

"It went through the black cupboard, so I guess it's in Endor, if that's its name."

"You shoved it through the cupboard?"

"No—"

"What happened to your hand?"

"Do you remember anything?" Henry asked.

"You plugged the toilet."

"After that."

"Oh." Henrietta furrowed her brow and looked around the room. "I looked through the black cupboard."

"And?"

"And the flashlight fell through."

"The flashlight? You were using a flashlight?"

"I taped it onto a yardstick and stuck it through next to the periscope."

"Are you stupid?"

Henrietta gave him a hard look. "That's not nice."

"You are! You're stupid!" Henry stood up and turned around in place. He pointed at her. "You're really, really dumb! Why would you do that?"

"Let me think," Henrietta said, glaring. "Oh, right. It was dark on the other side, and I wanted to see. Isn't that why people use flashlights?"

Henry couldn't stop moving. "And so you just stuck one into some strange, evil place, and it fell through."

"Yes. I did. Because I didn't run away scared, like you. I might be a girl, but you act more like one than I do."

Henry grunted.

"And it was my favorite," Henrietta said. "So when it fell, I reached in to see if I could find it. Do you think we could fish it back through?"

"No!" Henry yelled. "No! No! No!" He jumped. "No! You don't remember being grabbed? When I came upstairs, you were unconscious, up to your shoulder in the cupboard, face down on the floor. Someone was pulling you, and I had to reach in and stab them with my knife. No!"

Henrietta smiled and put her eyebrows up. "Really?" she said. "Well, if there is someone on the other side, it's not like they could do anything from in there. It's just a cut on your hand."

Now Henry was truly furious. He kicked the wall. He kicked the bed. He looked for something to throw. The cat sat by Henrietta and watched all of it. Henry almost said a lot of things, but his mouth and mind couldn't find them at the same time. He couldn't speak until he finally slowed down and stood breathing heavily.

"You're not allowed in my room," he said. "You're not allowed to look at my cupboards. You're not allowed to open them or talk to me about them. You are not allowed."

"It's not like I could open them if I'm not in your room," Henrietta said. She stood up and picked up the cat. "I think you're being silly," she said.

She knelt on Henry's bed and waddled across it to the doors. Without another word, she walked out of Henry's bedroom and down the stairs.

Henry flopped onto his bed, and his steam leaked slowly out. He began telling himself a story in his head. It was about how just and kind and understanding he

was. It was about how right he had been, how necessary his tone and word choice. It was about a girl who
just didn't understand, who was completely ignorant.
Then, for some reason, the narrator of the story in-
cluded an incident in which Henry had pushed an envelope into a strange place just to see what would
happen. It hadn't even been an accident. The incident
did not fit with the rest of the story, so Henry tried to
ignore it. He couldn't ignore it, so he tried to explain it.
Completely different things. The post office was obviously not dangerous. It was yellow. I just wanted to see
what the mailman would do. The flashlight was stupid.
I didn't shine a flashlight into the post office. She
didn't even act sorry. I would have acted sorry. I always
act sorry when people get upset. She didn't even care
that I probably saved her life. She didn't know. She was
unconscious. Oh, shut up.

Henry got to his feet and found a new shirt and
told himself to forget about it. When he walked downstairs, he made himself whistle. Henrietta was sitting at
the dining room table eating a sandwich.

"Yours is in the fridge," she told him.

"Thanks," Henry said, and went to find it. "Want a
drink?" he asked from the kitchen.

"Sure."

Henry came back out and sat down with his sandwich and two milks.

"I'm sorry I was stupid," Henrietta said. She reached up and tucked a loose strand of hair behind her ear, but she didn't look at him.

"I'm sorry I said you were stupid," Henry replied.

"I didn't mean to knock the flashlight in." Henrietta's voice was quiet.

Henry took a bite. "It was dumb to even have it."

"I said I was sorry," Henrietta muttered. "You would have done it if you hadn't been afraid."

Henry began to get angry and stopped himself. "It would have been just as stupid if I'd done it."

"And you would have," Henrietta said, finally looking at him.

Henry sniffed and spoke slowly. "I did not want to look in the black cupboard."

Henrietta stared back down at her plate. "But if you had wanted to, you would have used a flashlight."

"But I wouldn't have shoved it through," Henry said.

Both of them continued eating.

"I'm sorry I was stupid," Henrietta said again.

Henry took a deep breath. "I'm sorry I got mad and said you were stupid."

Henrietta pointed. "You should wash the blood off your hand. It's kind of gross, eating like that."

Henry shrugged. He hadn't washed for two reasons. First, because his fingers didn't hurt that much, and he thought that washing them might. Second, because he felt about ten years older every time he saw his bloody hand.

"We can finish putting all the names on the doors after lunch," Henrietta said.

"No," Henry said.

Henrietta looked at him. "What do you mean? I said I was sorry."

Henry stared at his sandwich. "I know. But I still don't want to do this. I don't want something bad to happen. We're not going to try and open any more."

"But I haven't even seen the post office yet," Henrietta said. "And what about Badon Hill? Those were both good places."

Henry thought about this. "Okay," he said. "Tonight you can come to my room and look in the yellow Byzanthamum place. But not till tonight, and I'm in charge." He looked at her. "You have to do what I say even if you don't want to."

It was Henrietta's turn to think. "Okay," she said.

"Good," Henry said into his glass. He took a long drink and thumped it back onto the table. "Don't ever open the black cupboard again."

Henrietta didn't say anything.

CHAPTER NINE

Henry spent the early afternoon covering the un-labeled cupboards with paper name tags. Henrietta had obviously wanted to come up to his room, but she just as obviously hadn't wanted to ask Henry's permission. As for Henry, he was in no mood to ex-tend an invitation. She would come tonight, and that was more than soon enough. He didn't know where Henrietta was or what she was doing, and he didn't care. Grandfather's key was in his pocket, and that meant she wasn't getting into any more trouble. She's probably in her room, Henry thought. Bored and angry. Or angry and bored.

He was right.

Occasionally Henry shivered and rubbed his still-chilled wrist or sucked on his knuckles. His body felt strange. He'd never experienced as much adrenaline as he had that morning, and now, with all of it gone and only cold memory remaining, shivers turned into wobbles and his joints felt soft.

Eventually Henry stood up and shook himself, knowing that he had to get out of his little room. Out of the house and into the sun. He nestled the key to the mailbox, Grandfather's key, the journal, the two confusing letters, and the postcard in a drawer, beneath his socks. He thought about telling Henrietta where he was going, but after a moment's hesitation near the landing, he moved on quietly. She could figure it out.

He walked into town and stopped at Zeke's house. Then he followed Zeke's mother's directions to the field where Zeke and his friends were playing. Henry joined in without fear. The sun was on his back and warmed his neck. The shivers were gone.

Henry was not the worst batter, nor was he the worst fielder. He was in a group of very average boys. Most were too lazy to do things right, and only a few diligently pursued proper technique at the plate or in the field. Zeke was one of those few, but he had long ago grown comfortable with the apathy that surrounded him—the perpetual foul balls, pop-ups, overthrows, and errors.

Henry successfully kept his mind on the game, which might seem strange for a boy who slept beside a wall of magic. But baseball was as magical to him as a green, mossy mountain covered in ancient trees. What's more, baseball was a magic he could run around in and laugh about. While the magic of the cupboards was not necessarily good, the smell of leather mixed with dusty sweat and spitting and running through sparse grass after a small ball couldn't be anything else.

Henry played until he was worried that his aunt and uncle would get home and wonder where he was. He made his farewells and started back through the empty, potholed streets of Henry, Kansas, toward the Willises' side of town. It was as far as he had ever walked by himself, and the freedom of it smelled as good to him as the mitt string he chewed on.

"Wait up!" Zeke's voice was followed by a whistle. Henry turned as Zeke jogged to catch up to him.

"Hey," Zeke said.

"Hey," said Henry.

Zeke swung his bat down from his shoulder and pushed his hat back on his head. "Thanks for coming out," he said. "We play most days. Come back."

"Sure," Henry said. "But I'm not great."

Zeke shrugged. "You see the ball. Most guys pull their heads. And you stayed on the breakers pretty good."

Henry glanced at his feet. "You struck me out three times."

Zeke laughed. "That's because you swing at cheese and can't get around on a fastball. Skip the stuff outside the zone, get a little bat speed, and you'll be fine." He started backing away. "Tomorrow?" he asked.

Henry nodded. "Sure."

"I'll come by and grab you for a little batting practice before we play." Zeke kicked the end of his bat and turned, whistling.

Henry watched him go, a little unsure of what exactly Zeke had meant by "cheese." Or "breakers." He wouldn't ask. He knew he would figure it out if he kept listening. It was probably obvious.

Henry moved on, and a few minutes later he stepped onto the Willises' road. Henry, Kansas, was to his right, miles of fields sprawled on his left, and half a mile ahead, the house sat in front of the looming barn. Henry's room and his wall crowded back into his mind. He glanced down at his hand. He had forgotten the cut across his knuckles.

Henrietta had already put Aunt Dotty's casserole in the oven and set the table. She smiled at Henry when he walked in and he smiled at her, but neither of them said anything. Henry climbed the stairs to the second floor and splashed water on his face in the bathroom. While he watched the muddy water splatter on the counter and swirl down the drain, the thunder of Uncle Frank's truck rattled the mirror. A minute later, Frank, Dotty, and the girls poured loudly in through the front door. Henry went downstairs to listen to his cousins describe the city.

After dinner, Henry climbed back up to his little attic bedroom. He stretched, then checked his sock drawer. At some point, Henrietta would come upstairs to look into the yellow Byzanthamum post office.

Blake the cat was sleeping at the end of the now-dry bed. Henry sat down beside him and ran the cat's tail through his hand, looking up at his identical posters. He was very used to the man who covered his wall. He knew every inch of his leg and thought his knee was strange. He didn't like his nose. Still, Henry appreciated him. The man was good at pretending that there weren't any cupboards in the wall behind him. He was much better at that than Henry was.

Henry sighed as he took the posters down, rolled the sheet the best he could, and shoved it in the corner. He stared at the cupboards and felt a little ill. Why was he going to let Henrietta mess around with things she didn't understand? And why was he always afraid? He hated being afraid.

At school, Henry had run away while a girl had her glasses stolen. He'd refused to jog a lap in PE because his ankle hurt. He remembered sitting on the top bunk of his bed, wanting to jump off but always using the stupid little ladder instead.

Henry pulled his bed as far away from the wall as

he could. There, looking up at him sideways, was the black cupboard door. Refusing to think about it, Henry bent over, grasped the cold metal knob, and pulled. The door popped off, and the short chain attached to the back rattled out behind it.

There, inside, was his knife, all clean and folded up. He got down on his knees and peered into the cupboard. There was nothing else—no flashlight, no shirt, no periscope.

He reached in and picked up his knife. Something tugged on it. He grabbed around behind the knife. A fine thread grazed his finger, so fine he could barely see it flicker in the lamplight. Henry pulled it and heard, very faintly on the other side, the sound of a small bell ringing.

Henry's throat tightened in panic. He jerked hard on the knife and heard the bell clatter in response. He jerked harder, and the thread broke.

Henry dropped to the floor, slammed the door back in place, kicked it tight, opened his knife, and sat on his bed panting. Blake now stood, with back arched and tail twitching. He stared at the little door, then looked at Henry.

"I know," Henry said. "I'm stupid." But he didn't mind. So what if someone knew that he'd gotten his knife back? What did it matter? He'd rung a bell on the other side. There was nothing they could do to him.

He forced himself to stay on his bed, resisting the impulse to drop to the floor and brace his feet against the small door. Instead, breathing heavily and waiting to hear Henrietta's footsteps on his staircase, he lay down with his head in the corner and turned off his light. He didn't let go of his knife. And he was glad when his other hand found Blake.

Nothing happened while Henry lay there. Nothing at all. And when anyone lies in the dark at the end of a long day with nothing happening, no matter how scared they might be, no matter how scared they are telling themselves not to be, they will eventually fall asleep. And Henry did.

The dream began, as many do, with a memory of sorts. Henry was in the upstairs bathroom. He was much younger, and the towels were a different color. He was also shorter, and he had cornered the cat. Blake was looking at him with his back to the bathtub. His white coat was the same, the gray spots were in all the same places, there just wasn't as much belly. Henry remembered what happened next. He remembered his final and surprising success as he dumped a towel full of cat into the toilet and tried to shut the lid. But he didn't get to see it again. The dream moved on.

His feet worked their way through thick, wet grass. Wind rolled around him; stars and an enormous orange moon hung over the tops of equally enormous tossing trees. Henry stopped. In front of him loomed the great slab of stone. Behind him, he knew, was the ancient cracked tree. For a brief moment, his waking mind processed another thought—through the tree behind him, he was sleeping in his bedroom. Then his dream self started doing something that hurt his foot. He was digging. He did not know where he had gotten the shovel, but his bare foot pressed against it, shoving the blade into the soft, mossy earth beside the stone. He pried, scooped, and tossed. In the grass beside him, the great black dog slept.

He did not dig long. When only a small hole had been dug, the shovel disappeared and he got down onto his hands and knees. Almost wondering why, but not quite, Henry shoved his head through the hole and into his bedroom. He was looking down on his room, his head sticking out of one of the higher cupboards. He couldn't tell which. His room was dark, but he could hear breathing. Even in his dream, Henry felt sick. Something cold was pulling at his insides. He knew the black cupboard was open. Something terrible was going to happen. He was asleep in bed and something horrible was coming. He tried to yell, to wake the breathing body below him. He tried to push through the cupboard, to drop in and wake himself, but his shoulders wouldn't fit. Something soft brushed his face. He tried to scream.

"Shhh." The voice was soft, only it wasn't a voice, it

was a thought inside his head. Someone was speaking inside his head. "You are strong, a dream walker and a pauper-son. But you left your body, and I can keep you out. You can watch yourself die."

Henry strained. His mind twisted and rolled, pushing out the voice.

He opened his eyes. He was flat on his back in his bed, breathing hard. His stomach was constricting up into his throat. He was going to throw up. Then a light flicked on. A very thin beam of light shone from the mailbox to a spot on one of his doors. Something soft brushed his cheek. He froze, only moving his head to look. A cat's tail curled before his face, switching from cheek to cheek. The cat was sitting on his chest. It was Blake. Blake was looking at something.

Henry leaned his head until he could just see past the cat. There was the mailbox with its small light, and near it, sitting on Henry's legs just above his knees, was something else. Something dark. Now that he could see it, he could feel its weight on his legs. Henry tried not to choke. Instead, he dropped his head back onto his pillow and reached over for his lamp. He flicked it on. The cat on his chest didn't move. Henry leaned his head around again and there, staring at Blake, was another cat. It was very thin. Where it had fur, it was black. On its shoulder and chest were large bare spots, red, furless, and infected sores.

The black cat shifted its eyes from Blake and stared at Henry. When it moved, Henry saw something else move as well. A small string was tied around its neck. The string ran off the bed toward the wall. Henry couldn't see, but he knew where it went. He knew which cupboard was open—his stomach and throat told him that—and he knew where the cat had come from. What he didn't know was what to do.

The cat on his chest tensed as the black cat stood up on Henry's legs. Henry heard a small rumbling from Blake. He wasn't hissing or spitting, he was growling, like a tiger would. Henry did not want a cat-fight on his chest. Neither did he want to sit up and knock Blake off. He couldn't kick, because the black cat was above his knees. Where was his knife? He must have dropped it. The black cat took another step forward.

Without deciding anything, Henry sat up, grabbed Blake to his chest with his right arm, and swung at the other cat with his left. He hit it. There was a high-pitched cat noise of pain as the cat flew off his bed toward his bedroom doors. Then the string pulled taut and the cat jerked in the air and dropped to the floor. With another jerk, the cat hit the side of Henry's bed and slid back to the top. It dug its claws into Henry's blanket and fought the string's pull. Henry watched the string strangle the panicked cat before the creature let go and hit the cupboards. For one second, its claws held on to the cupboard wall, and then it hit the floor. Henry jumped up, still clutching Blake, as the black cat was pulled, spitting, writhing, and clawing, back into the black cupboard. Henry held still for a moment, then dropped Blake and lunged for the cupboard door. He shoved it on as firmly as he could, then pushed the bed up against it.

Henry looked at Blake, white and gray and nonchalant. He was licking himself at the head of the bed. Blake glanced at Henry, then curled up on his pillow and closed his eyes.

CHAPTER TEN

Henry heard the attic stairs before his doors creaked open. Henrietta's eyes were wide, and she was grinning. She whispered as loudly as possible.

"Henry, I've found it! I found how to open more cupboards. Oh, Blake's in here. I didn't know you liked Blake."

Henry opened his mouth, but Henrietta didn't wait.

"I've found out everything!" She bounced up and down. "At least, I've found out something. I'll know more when I read more."

"You read Grandfather's journal?" Henry asked.

"No. I found another one. It was under his pillow."

"What?" Henry raised his eyebrows. "You went back into his bedroom? How?"

Henrietta smiled. "I used the key, of course. I came up and you were asleep and there wasn't any light in the mailbox, so I took the key and the journal."

"What?" Henry asked. "Why would you do that?"

"Well, I knew you wouldn't let me if you were awake." She laughed. "It's not like you had hidden them. They were in your sock drawer. That's the first place Anastasia always looks. Nobody hides things in a sock drawer unless they want them found."

"Henrietta—"

"Oh, just listen to me."

Henry stood up and put a finger to his lips.

"Fine," Henrietta whispered. "But listen. The journals are all about the cupboards. It says there are five that don't lock. We've only opened three, and one of those was locked, so there are three more. And it says something about going through the cupboards. I knew we could go through, I just don't understand it yet."

She dropped the old journal on Henry's bed and held open the new one. She pointed at a long list. "See? It has something to do with the compass locks. Each cupboard has a combination that you set on the compass locks, and then you go through."

"But it doesn't shrink you."

Henrietta laughed. "Well, it must, or the cupboard gets bigger. But let's open the other three before we try it. Oh!" She knelt on the bed to examine the cupboard wall. "The light's on in the mailbox."

"Yeah."

Henrietta looked at Henry. "Did you look through again?"

"No. Henrietta. Listen to me for a second." Henry took a deep breath and described what had happened with the sick cat.

Henrietta cocked her head. "Are you sure you were awake?"

"Yes. I was dreaming, but when I woke up, both cats were on me."

"That was very nice of Blake," Henrietta said. "You know he doesn't like you." She looked at the wall. "They can open doors from the other side? How?"

"Well, the black one just pushes on and off. It doesn't have a latch. I pushed the bed up against it."

"How did you know the cat was sick?"

"It had big sores and bald spots."

"Oh." Henrietta wrinkled up her nose. "That's gross, Henry."

"Yeah," Henry said. "I think it was trying to get to my face, but I don't know."

Henrietta shook her head. "Don't tell me any more. Just keep the bed against it, and don't open it again."

Henry felt his ears getting hot. "What do you mean, don't open it again? You're the one who always wants to open it."

"It just came open?" Henrietta asked. "You didn't open it first?"

Henry paused.

"Well, I did, and my knife was in it. I took it out and

then closed the door." He didn't mention the string and the bell ringing on the other side.

"See?" Henrietta said. "Whoever it is on the other side put your knife there to see if you opened it again. So just don't open it again. Now, let's try to find the other ones that open."

Henry flopped back onto his bed, trying hard not to be irritated. "Don't you want to look in the post office first?" he asked.

"Sure."

Henrietta bounced over to the little door while Henry got the key out of his dresser to open it for her. Henrietta watched for a long time, but the legs walked by only once.

"That's neat, but let's do the other ones now." Henrietta looked over the wall, reading the numbers she had taped on each cupboard. "Numbers 24, 49, and 3 are the ones. Look, 24 and 49 are right here, close to each other, but 3 is all the way at the other end. I wish they were all in order. I wonder why they aren't."

Henry was already examining the cupboard labeled "24." Its name was "Cleave," and its surface was a rough, darker wood. There was no latch anywhere and no keyhole.

"Does the book say how to open it?" Henry asked. "There's nothing on the door."

"Try hitting it."

Henry made a fist and thumped the door. Nothing happened. He felt around its edges. Small hinges were on the right side. At the top, his fingers found a groove. It still had loose plaster in it. He cleared it out with his fingertips, then pulled.

The door opened with a pop and a cloud of dust. The small cupboard looked empty, but the back was hidden in darkness.

"Nothing," Henry said.

"Reach inside."

Henry thought about saying something nasty. Instead, he stuck his hand in the cupboard and felt around.

"There's a back," Henry said. "It doesn't go anywhere."

"Push on it." Henrietta stood up on the bed next to him and leaned in.

"You're breathing on me," Henry said.

"Oh well."

"It smells awful."

"Oh well," Henrietta said again.

Henry was straining against the back of the cupboard. He thought he felt it budge, so he bore down and pushed harder. The bed began sliding away from the wall.

Suddenly the back of the cupboard gave, and Henry smacked his face on the wall as his arm went all the way through. His fingers, in some other place, closed around a fistful of hair. The head that owned it jerked and yelled. Henry let go and jumped back.

Henrietta was sitting on the bed, shivering. "Henry! Shut it! Quick!"

Henry started to.

"No, the other one," Henrietta said. "Over there. Something just reached through and grabbed me." Henry looked back at the wall. Two cupboards were open—24 was the one he had just been reaching in, but 49, just above it and to the right, was also open.

"Oh my goodness," Henry said, and he laughed.

"Why are you laughing? Shut it!" Henrietta stood up to do it herself. Henry reached back into number 24. His hand came out of 49 and grabbed at Henrietta's face. She stifled a scream and slammed the door on it. Henry yelped and fell back down on the bed, sucking his knuckles and laughing. Henrietta looked down at him with her fists on her hips.

"Why are you laughing?"

Henry answered with more half-stifled laughter.

"Was that your hand?" she asked. "It wasn't funny if it was."

"Yeah, it was," he said, and sat up grinning. "It was really funny. You should have seen your face."

"I hope I hurt your hand."

"Not bad."

Henrietta turned back to the wall. "How does that work?"

"I guess the two cupboards are connected," Henry said. "Anything that goes in one comes out the other." Henry jumped back up. He forced his face into a serious expression before shoving his left arm into the cupboard as far as it would go. Most of his arm came out of the other cupboard. He reached over and began to feel his own face, then bugged his eyes at Henrietta. He spread his fingers and reached for her.

"It's coming," he said.

"Stop it."

"It's coming!" he said, and twiddled his fingers.

"Stop it!" she said, and slapped his hand. But she was smiling now. "That is really weird."

"Let's do it with Blake," Henry said.

"Don't be mean to the cat."

"It's not mean. It'll just be funny."

Blake had long since removed himself from the bed and was sitting by the door.

"C'mere, Blake," Henry said. He hopped off the bed and scooped up the cat. "Do you want to do magic?" He held the cat up to the lower open cupboard.

"Don't make him if he doesn't want to." But Blake didn't mind. The cupboard didn't seem at all unusual to him. He stepped in, and almost immediately his head emerged from the upper cupboard while his tail twisted and swung from the lower. He seemed to have found just the sort of spot that he enjoyed. He turned his head back and forth, then lay down and began licking his paw.

"He likes it," Henrietta said.

"Of course he does, it's hilarious," said Henry. "Where's the other one? Was it number 2?"

"It's 3, all the way at the other end, by the corner."

The two of them left Blake contentedly halved and scrambled to door number 3. Its paper tag said "Mistra." The door was smaller than most, and darker. It wasn't black, it just seemed dirty. Henry was wondering how he would clean it when Henrietta spat on it. She picked one of Henry's T-shirts up off the floor and began rubbing.

"You should take your laundry down, or Mom will come up to get it," she said while she scrubbed.

"I take it down all the time," Henry said. "And I bring it back up."

Henrietta raised her eyebrows. "Sheets?"

"What do you mean?"

"Have you taken your sheets down?"

Henry nodded. "Once."

"Mom's doing sheets tomorrow. Oh, look."

Henry already was. Silver inlay swirled around the

edges of the door, then stretched toward the middle in what looked like branches. In the center was a half-dollar-sized circle.

"Do you have your knife?" Henrietta asked. "You got it out of the black cupboard, didn't you?"

"Yeah."

Henrietta looked at him. "Where is it?"

"Why?" Henry asked.

"I need it."

"What for?"

"Just give it to me." Henrietta turned back to the door.

"Fine." Henry crawled over the bed, found the knife on the floor, and brought it to Henrietta. She pushed the blade under the smooth metal circle in the door and it popped up. Underneath was a metal ring. She hooked a finger through it and pulled.

"It's a drawer," she said. And it was. The drawer slid out, and they both scootched back. Henrietta pulled it all the way out, set it on the floor, and bent over to look in the hole. It was too dark, so she reached in and fished around with her hand. Her eyes narrowed.

"What is it?" Henry asked.

"I think it's warmer. I can't really feel anything else."

"What's in the drawer?"

They looked together. There was an old and

tattered cloth, some nearly-dust mouse droppings, small bones next to gray shards of what must have been skin, two dead beetles, and a fly.

"Well, that's a little boring," she said. "What do we do now?"

"Go to sleep?" Henry asked.

"No. We have to try the compass locks." She moved to the edge of the bed and spun one of the knobs before looking around for the journal. She picked up the one on the blanket and set it back down. "Did you put the other one somewhere?"

"No. You had it."

"I know I had it, but did you take it?"

Henry snorted. "Why would I take it?"

"I don't know. Did you?"

"No."

On the floor below them, something thumped. Both children froze.

"Oh no," Henrietta whispered.

"What is it?"

"I think Dad's awake."

"Maybe he's just going to the bathroom," Henry said.

Henrietta looked at him and smiled nervously. "But I left Grandfather's room open."

"What?"

"And the light on."

"Why?"

"Because I was excited about the journal. I ran right up here."

"Well, hurry up and go turn the light off and shut the door," Henry said. "And if your dad catches you, then tell the truth."

Henrietta jumped up and ran out of the room on her toes. Henry listened to her feet on the stairs, waiting for Frank's voice. There was more thumping, and Blake ran out of the room. Henry stood up and looked at the compass knobs. He fiddled with them, twisting each and trying to watch all of the doors at once to see if anything happened.

Nothing. The doors were still. The floor below him was still. No creaks, no voices, no sounds. No Henrietta. Henry waited. He waited until he knew it had been too long and then, suddenly, he worried.

He walked down the stairs as softly as he could. At the bottom, he listened but didn't hear anything, so he stepped onto the landing. Blake was gone, Grandfather's door was open, and the light was still on. Henry walked slowly across the landing, past the girls' room and Aunt Dotty and Uncle Frank's room and then the bathroom. He stepped over the mess in the floor and looked into Grandfather's room.

The door was only halfway open, so he could see just a slice of the space. He moved closer and peered around the door, an inch at a time. No one. Some of the books were on the floor. That could account for the thumping. And then, as he stepped all the way into the room, he saw something that he understood far better than he wished.

A cupboard door, beneath and beside Grandfather's bookshelf, was open. The opening was small, but big enough for a person to fit through. The light from the room didn't seem to penetrate it. On the floor outside the door was a shoe and half a pair of glasses. They weren't Henrietta's.

Henry knew what kind of cupboard this must be, and he suddenly understood how someone had been able to live in the house unseen. He knew what he should do. He should go wake up Uncle Frank, hand over the journals and the keys, tell him everything, and apologize.

Instead, he dropped onto his hands and knees, took a deep breath, and crawled into the cupboard.

CHAPTER ELEVEN

Henry's eyes were shut, and he expected, once he opened them, to find himself in another place. Instead, he ran into the back of the cupboard. He squirmed his way out and sat on the floor, confused and rubbing his head.

It was the middle of the night, he was in Grandfather's bedroom, and Henrietta was missing. Henry examined the shoe and the broken gold-rimmed glasses. He was not the Henry who would have sat there two weeks ago. He didn't once tell himself that Henrietta was probably down in the kitchen or in the bathroom. He knew she had gone through the cupboard, and he thought that someone else, someone he may have seen, had gone with her. Or taken her.

Henry was worried, and his heart was trying to fly in his chest. He was worrying that he wouldn't figure out how to follow Henrietta through the cupboard before she got hurt, and that he might not be able to get her back before her parents woke up.

He got onto his hands and knees and felt his way back into the cupboard. There was nothing inside but a funny smell and the solid back. Henry climbed out and began pulling at various books on the shelves around the cupboard, hoping one would trigger a mechanism and open the back. None of them did. He pushed on every bit of wood that looked secretive, and still nothing happened.

Henry walked to the door. He didn't want to leave the room, but he needed to find the journal Henrietta had been reading. He went as quietly as he could to his room. Once there, he moved the old journal and rifled through his blanket, shoved aside his posters, and then dropped to the floor to look under his bed. There it was—open, face down, some of the pages bending. He pulled the journal out without looking at it and hurried back downstairs. He sat on the floor beside the cupboard and looked at the first page. His eyes struggled with the handwriting but began to adjust after several lines. He skimmed over it as quickly as he could.

> To Frank and Dorothy,
> I have written all that I know about the cupboards in this book. In my other journal, there are some helpful things that I will not repeat here for the sake of time, as I

would prefer to have finished this before I am dead, though I may not. The doctors would bury me now, and my body seems to agree, as it already turns to dust. Here also, I intend to be as honest as I have always been deceptive, though honesty will no doubt damage your memory of me.

The cupboards were first assembled by my father, and the process was the work of his life. I have, after struggling through his papers, assembled the stories behind each of his acquisitions and his choice of this place for his house. The cupboards' functions vary a great deal, shifting because of grains, origins, etc. Some allow the passage of light, some of sound, and some remain as dark and silent as tombs.

Of course, the house was designed after his studies and was meant, for many reasons, to culminate in the cupboards. There are things he did not discover until much later and things he would have changed, like the location of the primary entrance (he could never get one to work on the same wall as the cupboards, or even the same floor), but he never had the energy to attempt a second house design.

I have restructured and rebuilt the house as much as I was able and opened the last of the cupboards.

I will attempt to explain how things function as they are. I do this not because I would recommend that you exploit your access to these places, but because my father ran great risks and was damaged in many ways for the entirety of his life as a result of his experiments, studies, and exploration. He left me to undergo the same process, making the same discoveries, though I was able to avoid much through a careful reading of his notes. While I would not recommend you attempt any exploration, neither can I tell you not to without hypocrisy, something you may be surprised to hear, as hypocrisy was at times natural to me. I understand that the cupboards cannot remain hidden forever and can hardly expect that you have forgotten them, as memories such as the ones you formed as children are not easily struck from the mind's page. You will rediscover the cupboards, and you will find it necessary to explore them. This is written so that you may avoid harm, such *as is possible in such undertakings, but particularly the mistakes made by my father and myself.*

Henry turned the page, glanced at it, and then, impatient, flipped to the middle somewhere and began reading again.

I cannot explain it, and though he was first and foremost a mathematician, he was never able to come up with a stable formula for the passage of time in a cupboard relative to the passage of time here. His journals are littered with attempts. He found that time passed differently through each of them, at varying and apparently inconsistent rates. This by itself accounts for much of my father's sickness, or so he thought. For myself, as I so early chose only one to pass through, I did not experience nearly the temporal upheaval that he did. And, of course, after my first experience, I never traveled without the rope, which I have always left coiled beneath the bed. It is not necessary for one with magic, but it was woven "elsewhere" and aids the mind of the weaker traveler.

Henry stood up and walked over to the bed. Beneath it was a pile of brown rope with one end tied to the bed leg. He sat on the edge of the bed, flipped toward the back of the book, and found the page Henrietta had shown him—a list of the cupboards, each one next to a compass-lock combination. He flipped back a couple of pages.

Of course, many combinations lead nowhere. They might, if additional cupboards were found and aligned, but they do not now. When the locks are set to any of these empty combinations, the back of the main cupboard will be as solid as any other. Nothing could pass through it, because it terminates in our own space. The benefit of this, as I quickly learned, was that no thing could pass through from the other direction, either. I could go nowhere, but I also would not wake to find myself sharing a room with a noble-hog, as happened to me twice. Before I set the compass locks permanently to what would become my second place, I would never sleep unless the locks were set to an empty combination and the back of my cupboard was solid. This, of course, does not prevent *things from entering the cupboards in the attic. But they would need to be very small and also strong enough to force the door open from the inside (the most startling variation on this was the boy Henry).*

Henry coughed and read the line again. There he was, a simple parenthetical, an offhand comment. His eyes flew back over the words and hurried on, hoping for some kind of elaboration.

Once I had permanently set the combination with plaster, I would still frequently wedge the door shut when I was not using it. I have copied all the combinations for the cupboards in the next pages. When one of their combinations has been set, you will find no back to my cupboard. The back is still there, as is the wall that supports it, but the cupboard meets with another place before it meets with the wall.

Henry sat very still. There were no answers to the questions flooding his mind, but he had found the mechanism of the cupboards. He did not know how it worked or why, but he believed that it would.

It was very late. He wanted to read both journals

from front to back to front. He wanted to know exactly who he was and where he came from. But Henrietta had disappeared. He had no time.

Henry knew what he had to do next. He was going to go upstairs and guess which cupboard Henrietta had gone through. Then he was going to crawl through a small door in his dead grandfather's bedroom. He might be crawling home and not know it. He might crawl into some place worse than Endor.

He felt strange leaving his grandfather's room. He didn't shut the door, because Henrietta still had the key. He didn't turn the light off, because he didn't want to come back to a dark room. When he reached the attic, he sat down on his bed and stared at the compass locks. If he understood what the journal had been saying, the combination that he set would determine which cupboard, or place, he would go to when he crawled through the larger cupboard downstairs. Henrietta had turned a knob before they heard the thumping, so the combination must have let something through. Henrietta had gone downstairs to turn the light off and shut the door to Grandfather's room. Whatever it was must have taken her back through the cupboard.

"Or she followed it," he muttered out loud.

And then Henry had turned the knobs again while

he was waiting, after she'd gone downstairs. That's why the cupboard was closed.

Henry's chin crept toward his chest. He felt his jaw tense. His eyes watered a bit and then shut completely as he yawned, a long, sprawling yawn. He wasn't tired. He certainly wasn't bored. He was nervous, more nervous than he had ever been. He yawned again. He took slow, deep breaths, but they weren't enough. His body kept yawning, his hands were cold, and his spine prickled. At least he wasn't panicking or throwing up. Yet.

He stood up to look at the compass locks and hoped that the combination for the cupboard Henrietta had gone through would be fairly close to the one the knobs were set to now. He looked at the strange figures around the two knobs, then looked at his grandfather's journal. He found a combination four figures off from the knob on the left and two from the one on the right. He checked the number of the cupboard and found it on his wall. It was a normal-looking brown one. Its name tag said "Tempore."

Before Henry set the combination, he made sure he had his knife. He pulled his backpack out from under the bed and tucked both of Grandfather's journals inside it. He slid his arms through the straps and turned to the compass locks.

With a deep breath, he carefully twisted the knobs.

In Grandfather's room, he shut the door most of the way and stared at the still-open cupboard. He went to the bed and pulled out the rope. He figured that the rope was supposed to be tied to the bed leg, so he just held the loose end. Then he turned off the light.

Henry stood in the dark for a moment to let his eyes adjust, then he got down on his knees in front of the small door. His knife was in one hand and the rope in the other. He didn't fit very well with his backpack on, but he dropped to his belly and squirmed in.

A loud ticking surrounded him. The smell of a wood fire.

Henry worked his way farther in, and the ticking grew louder. He could see a room now, but firelight was reflecting off something in front of him.

He was behind glass.

Henry pushed on it and felt it bend. He tried to look above himself, but he was squeezed in too tight to turn. So he just pushed his head up. The top of the cupboard was gone. He put his forehead on the glass and tried to pull his legs in behind him. They came a little ways, so he moved his head higher and tried to work his way closer to vertical. The ticking was very loud now, though he wasn't paying much attention to it.

He bumped his head on something heavy. Something else chopped at the back of his scalp. He yelped and tried to drop back down but only banged his head again. Noise filled the small space—rattling and bonging as chimes shook and met each other above his head.

I'm in a clock, Henry thought.

Something was moving in the room. It had stepped in front of the fire. Henry froze. It was walking toward him. Henry heard a voice on the other side of the glass. It was a boy's voice.

"What are you doing?" it said.

"Um . . . ," Henry said, and tried to shift his weight.

"Why are you in the clock?"

Henry grunted. "I'm stuck."

"Where's the rest of you?"

"It's stuck, too."

The boy laughed. "But how did you get in there? How do you fit?"

"I don't." Henry heard a click, the glass pressing against his face moved, and his head fell forward. He levered himself with his elbows and squirmed out onto the floor. Then he looked up at a skinny, white-faced boy. He noticed first that the boy's lips were large and second that his pants were pulled very high, up to his ribs. The legs only reached the middle of his shins.

"They always leave the key in it," the boy said. "You would have been locked in if they didn't. How did you get in there?"

Henry looked back at the clock. It was a grandfather clock, big but not enormous. The pendulum had already forgotten it had clipped Henry's head and was swinging steadily. The weights were still shifting and bumping into each other.

"I came through from the other side," Henry said.

"Is it a secret room?"

"No. I don't really know how it works."

"A tunnel?"

"No. The back of the clock just connects to somewhere else."

"Is it magic?"

Henry wasn't listening. He was looking around the room. The fireplace was wide, built from smooth stone, and a low, bulging couch and matching chairs squatted in front of it. One wall looked like it might be entirely windows but was covered with heavy purple curtains.

"Is it night?" Henry asked, sitting up.

"No," the boy said. "Just winter."

"What do you mean?"

"I'm not allowed to open the drapes. They're supposed to keep the room warmer. I've been in here all day. They don't let me out, usually."

"Who doesn't?"

"Well, Annabee mostly. She brings me my meals, though. Most times. I'm going to have her sacked when I've grown."

"Has a girl come through here?" Henry asked. He already knew the answer.

"Through the clock?"

"Yeah."

"Today?"

"Yeah."

"Well, it wouldn't have mattered if you'd said yesterday. You're the first one ever to come through the clock that I know of."

Henry clicked his tongue and looked around. "I bet my grandfather did."

"Was he a wizard?"

"No. I don't know what he was. He called this place Tempore in his journal."

"We call it Hutchins."

Henry looked at the smaller boy. "I have to go now. I need to find my cousin. I don't know where she went."

"Might she come through the clock?"

Henry looked at the small clock cabinet. "I don't think so. Anyway, I have to go." He stepped back to the clock and looked in. The rope hung out the bottom.

"What's your name?" the boy asked.

Henry didn't look back. "Henry," he said.

"Mine's Richard. What's your surname?"

Henry thought about this for a moment.

"York," he said.

"Henry York? Is your father the admiral?"

"No," Henry said. "I don't know who my father is."

"Oh." Richard stepped just beside Henry. "Mine's dead. That's why the others all have to look after me."

"Sorry."

"My mother's run off." The boy bent over and looked in the clock. "My surname is Leeds, though I'm going to change it."

"Sorry," Henry said again. "I really have to go."

"Right."

Henry got down on his hands and knees and crawled into the clock. There was a back to it. Henry's head pushed against it, and he went nowhere. He sat back up and took a deep breath to prevent panic. Richard watched as Henry closed his eyes, reached into the clock, gripped the rope with his left hand, and felt his way along it. To Richard's eyes, Henry was crawling through solid wood. His shoulders disappeared as the backpack seemed to catch on something. Henry's legs lowered themselves, and the pack vanished, followed by Henry's legs and feet. Then the rope vanished as well.

Henry ran up the attic stairs, no longer trying to dodge the creaks and squeals of the old treads. He pulled the journal out of his backpack and dropped onto his bed in front of the compass locks.

"Faster this time," he whispered to himself, flipping to the back of the journal, looking for the combinations. When he found them, he scanned the list and glanced up at the compass locks. The closest combination belonged to another small door, though made of a darker wood than Tempore's. The name tag, in Henrietta's handwriting, said "Carnassus."

Henry set the compass locks and hurried back down to Grandfather's room with his backpack on and his knife in his hand. He was very careful not to close the door all the way behind him. He didn't want to be locked in.

"You *would* take the key with you, wouldn't you, Henrietta?" Panic was knocking somewhere in Henry's mind, and he was trying to ward it off with irritation. "After stealing it from my drawer. Sock drawers are not public property."

Nervous again and blowing out long breaths, he walked straight to the cupboard, grabbed the end of the rope, did not notice that the cupboard door was open when he had left it shut, and crawled in.

He didn't know what he would be crawling into, so he inched his face along, waiting for something to become visible. That something was a stone floor, cold beneath his hands.

Stone walls stood close to him on both sides. A wooden arch joined the two sides, an arch filled with a heavy black curtain. Henry pulled himself to his knees and glanced around. The whole space was about the size of a closet. The walls weren't more than four feet apart, the curtain about six feet from the back. The only light was coming in above and beneath the curtain. It was a cold white light, but bright enough.

Henry stood up, stepped toward the curtain, and tried to look around it. It was piled up against the stone walls on both sides, so he hooked one edge with his finger and eased it back far enough for his eye.

He saw the moon. At first, that's all he saw. Its large white face filled a window high on a wall. He did not know that the window, which was actually more of a light well, had been built to cast its light—on one day of the year and in the night's middle—upon the dark curtain in front of him. He did not realize, at least for a moment, that the moon lit the black curtain and very little else. He drew the curtain farther back and looked around the room.

A huge gong rolled through the chamber, vibrating Henry's bones. Something bumped him from behind. He jumped, stepped on his own foot, twisted, and fell out through the curtain and onto the floor. He'd dropped his knife.

"That way," an old voice said, "has been closed for many years."

The gong's echoes were still dying. Henry didn't say anything. He didn't stand up. He looked around for the voice, running his hands over the stone for his knife.

"Name yourself," the voice said.

Henry didn't respond. His hand closed on the knife handle. Turning to where he thought the voice was coming from, he pushed off the ground and stood up. He gripped his small defense tight.

"Name yourself," the voice said again.

This time, Henry answered. "I can't," he said.

The old voice laughed and said something Henry couldn't understand. The sounds made his blood tingle and his cheeks hot.

Suddenly the room woke. Torches and trays burst into flame all around the walls.

Henry blinked. The room was an oval. At one end, steps led down into a hall. At the other sat a black polished dais. It was all square, cut with hard lines and no curves. On it, carved from the same stone, was a square-edged chair with arms but no back. A wrinkled bundle of cloth sat upon it.

Black curtains hung at intervals all around the walls in arches like the one Henry had come through. Between them, stands that looked like they should hold fake ferns instead held the trays of flame.

"If you choose to pick at words," the voice said, "what is it that others named you?"

"York," Henry said.

"This is not a room for lies." The bundle on the dais took shape, straightening, growing, and then leaning forward. An old man wrapped in black cloth stared at Henry. A long white beard grew off the tip of his chin, and a thick neck stood out behind it. His hair was pulled tight to his skull. Except for his head, the man was small. His eyes were fixed on Henry's face. "Your name is not York," he said softly.

Henry shifted his feet. "My father is Phillip Louis York," he said.

"Your father was never called York. I have seen him here before. No other ever came unbidden." The man held a smooth shaft of wood in his left hand. His right hung over the arm of his chair into a bowl. He lifted up something white and moving, pinched between his fingers. Then he put it in his mouth and smiled.

Henry clenched his fists. "Did you take my cousin? I'm looking for her."

The old man laughed. "Is she missing? Are you

missing? Will she come to look for you? Or will it be your father? How is it that you found the way?"

"I don't know which way it was," Henry said. "There are lots of them."

The man pointed his staff at Henry. "You do not know of many ways. You cannot. You are too young. The magic would collapse you."

"I do," Henry said, and felt around his memory, trying to see the list from his grandfather's journal. "I know the way to Tempore. I have been there tonight. I know the way to . . . Mistra, to Badon Hill, and to Byzanthamum. I know the way to Arizona." The man leaned even farther forward, his eyes hooded.

Henry grabbed for more, hoping the stranger wouldn't know the difference. "And Boston, Florida, Kansas, Vermont, Mexico, Africa, and New York." The man still looked at him, stiff and expressionless.

"I know the way to Endor," Henry said, and saw surprise register on the old man's face.

"Did your father tell you these names?"

"My grandfather wrote of them."

"Tell me, what is this place called? I do not think many know that."

"Carnassus," Henry said.

The old man sat very still before he spoke again. "Where did your grandfather write these things?"

"In a book I have," Henry said. "At home," he lied.

"Where is home?"

Henry didn't want to say Kansas again.

"Henry," he said.

"Henry?"

"It is a place called Henry."

"And you came from Henry to this place. How long did it take you?"

"Not long. I should go back now. I still need to find my cousin."

The man sat back, lifted more from the bowl, and chewed slowly. "I did not think you would come. I believed the door was lost and would never reopen, despite the old words. And I have others to content me. But now that you have come, I cannot let you leave."

"I need to find my cousin."

"She is not here."

Henry stepped back toward the black curtain.

"Doors can shut on both sides," the man said. "You will not find it open."

Henry pulled back the curtain. Richard stood just inside looking terrified.

"Sorry I bumped you," Richard whispered.

Henry didn't know what to say. He had been planning on diving through and running straight up to the compass locks before he could be followed. But he couldn't leave Richard behind. He looked down at the floor and saw the rope.

"Go back right now," he said. And he shut the curtain.

"The way is closed?" the old man asked. "You will be allowed to leave when we have talked more about your book. I will not keep you long. I do not want your father returning." The man laughed. "It is strange that I did not know of all his sons. Of course, to have only six would have been a grief to him. I should have known there would be a seventh."

"I'm an only child," Henry said. But he didn't really know anymore. Not after what he'd read. He heard footsteps and looked back at the hall. Two men were climbing the steps, both holding staffs. Henry let his knife fall open and gripped it tight behind his leg. They walked toward him with extended arms and began a low chant.

Heaviness drifted over Henry like a lazy breeze. They came closer and repeated the process. It felt heavier this time, but also seemed to pass right through him. They stopped in front of him, and one of them pulled a long knife out of his robe and waved it, muttering. The other one reached for Henry.

Henry brought his little blade around hard. The two men jumped back. The man with the knife tripped and fell over. Henry hit the other one in the head, but with his fist more than the knife. Then he dove behind the curtain and was grateful to find Richard gone. He scrambled to his knees and crawled as quickly as he could, one hand on the rope, back to Grandfather's bedroom. Once there, he rolled out on the floor, jerked the rope through, and shut the door. Richard stood beside him, his mouth open.

"Be very quiet," Henry said, and handed him the knife. "Don't let anyone through. I'll be right back." Henry ran out of the room on his toes and straight up his stairs. Once he'd set the compass locks to an empty combination, he tiptoed as quickly as he could back downstairs. Richard was waiting for him, looking moon-pale.

"A hand pushed the door open, and I kicked it." Richard pointed. "I shut the door again."

Henry squatted down, opened the cupboard slowly, and looked inside. The hand sat by itself near the back. There wasn't any arm.

"Oh no," Henry said.

"What?" Richard asked, and bent over to look.

Henry took a deep breath. "I cut his hand off."

"How?"

"When I switched the cupboard."

Richard looked at him. "What are you going to do with it?"

Henry thought for a moment. "I think I should give it back."

"Well, it's not your fault."

"I know," Henry said, "but I don't want to have to go bury it in the backyard or something. Maybe they could put it back on. Listen. You sit down here, and I'll go switch the cupboard back. I'll only leave it there a second. As soon as you can't see the back of the cupboard, push the hand through with your foot, okay? It'll only be a second, so go fast."

"Hold, uh, hold on, are you sure?" Richard asked.

"Yeah. Get ready." Henry left the room again and creaked his way back up the stairs. He was sure he would probably wake somebody up, but he didn't care right now. He took a deep breath in front of the cupboards, then set the knobs back to Carnassus. He counted to two, turned the knobs again, and went back downstairs. He didn't hear any yelling, so he thought it had probably worked.

"That was disgusting," Richard said.

"Did it work?"

"Yes, but you nicked the tip off my boot." Henry looked down at Richard's delicate leather shoe. At the very end, a slice had taken about an eighth of an inch off the toe. He looked back at Richard.

"Why did you follow me? You have to go back."

"Why?"

"Because you can't stay here."

"Why not?"

"Well," Henry said, "because nobody here knows that I can go to other places, and my cousin is missing, and I have to find her tonight. She could be in big trouble, and even if she isn't, we'll still get into trouble."

"I'll look for her with you." Richard reached up and pulled nervously at his thick lower lip.

Henry shook his head. "You have to go back."

"I don't see why," Richard said, and went over and sat on the bed. "Who sleeps in here?"

"Nobody asked you to come," Henry said.

"Nobody asked you to come into my clock. I could have left you in there, you know. Who sleeps in here?"

"It was my grandfather's room." Henry crossed his arms. "He's dead. Nobody sleeps in here now."

"Then I'll stay in here." Richard smiled. "You don't have to tell your parents."

"It's my aunt and uncle's house."

"You don't have to tell them."

"No," said Henry.

Richard sniffed. "Well, at least let me look for your cousin," he said. "I'll go back at the end of the night."

Henry stared at the boy's pasty face.

"I don't get to do anything," Richard said. "And I'm staying even if you say I can't."

Henry sighed. "Okay." He pointed at the skinny boy. "But you have to do what I say."

"Fine," Richard said, and grinned. Henry didn't like his teeth.

"Okay. C'mon, then," Henry said. "We have to go upstairs and pick our next place. Be quiet. Everyone else is asleep. And don't close the door." Henry left the room and went to the stairs without looking back. He heard Richard trip slightly on the torn carpet, but he ignored it. In his room, he pulled the journal out of his backpack and looked for the next close combination. When he found it, he almost laughed. He hoped he would find Henrietta there, and if he did, he knew he would have trouble bringing her back. He was going to take Richard to Badon Hill.

Henry set the combination and told Richard not to ask any questions, and not to touch the doors, and not to make so much noise with his feet.

Richard tried very hard not to ask any questions as he stood in the strange bedroom and watched Henry crawl through the cupboard. And he did very well, though he followed much closer than Henry had told him to and kept reaching out to make sure that Henry's feet were still there.

At the back of the cupboard, Henry felt himself going up. He felt earth under his closed fists, and then he felt grass. He dragged the rope along with him and squeezed out of the tree and into the air. The sky was enormous and lower than any sky he had seen. He looked back at the tree. The trunk hulked, but the crack didn't look large enough to crawl through. Then he saw Richard's head and blinking eyes emerge from the wood, and he laughed. He was actually on Badon Hill. The sun was bright, though low, and the breeze-blown grass stroked the sides of the tall gray stone and just hid the bones that Henry knew were there. Then something jumped up and scrambled onto the rock, in front of the sun. Henry had to squint to make it out.

"Blake!" he said, and laughed even more. "Richard, she's here. She has to be. Come on!"

Richard was still blinking, but he could see the cat and the sky and the grass and the tops of huge, wind-lazy trees, and it was all beautiful. Henry was bigger than he was, so he didn't want to cry in front of him. He stood up and closed his eyes. "I like it here," he said.

Henry was standing on the stone, holding Blake. Richard tried to climb up beside him but couldn't quite make it. Henry reached down and gave him a pull.

The two of them stood and looked out over the woods.

"There's a lot more of the mountain than I thought," Henry said. "And a funny smell."

Blake jumped out of his arms and off the rock.

"It's the sea," Richard said. He pointed to a blue expanse partially hidden by the treetops. "I've smelled it once before. You can see the water over there. We're very high. Is it an island?"

"I don't know," Henry said. "But we should go. Henrietta's got a head start on us."

Henry got off the rock and almost tripped on the cat. Blake stood at his feet and stared blankly at him. Then the cat ran, as much as Blake ever ran, over to the crack in the tree and disappeared, only to reemerge and stare at Henry again. Then he ran back to the crack.

"The cat wants to go back," Richard said.

"We'll go back in a bit, Blake. We've got to find Henrietta first." Henry turned and began walking down the slope to an old broken wall. Richard followed him. Blake passed them both, leapt onto the rubble of the wall, and arched his back, hissing at Henry.

"Stop it, Blake," Henry said. He put his hand on the wall to jump over but pulled it back quickly, bleeding. Blake crouched, quietly now, but he had left four deep claw tracks across the back of Henry's hand.

"Blake!" Henry yelled. "Fine! Shoo! Go home or whatever, but we've got to find Henrietta." He pressed his cut hand to his lips.

Richard shifted nervously next to Henry. "Perhaps she's not here," he said.

"If the cat's here, she's here," Henry said. "Easy enough."

"Is it possible that the cat may have followed us?" Richard asked.

Henry sighed. He couldn't be irritated. Frustration turned to despair. Richard could be right, and if Richard was right, then Henrietta might be lost forever. He turned to Blake. "I wish you were a dog," he said. "Where's Henrietta?" He whistled. "Find Henrietta!"

Blake looked insulted, but he hopped off the wall with his gray tail in the air and began walking back to the tree.

Henry pulled in as much of the Badon air as he could manage and listened to the breeze roll and toss too many leaves to count. The air moved gently, but the sound of its leaf passage was strong and constant, like many waters. It felt right on his face. He could smell the moss and the soft earth and sunshine. His bones tingled with—with—he didn't know what. Magic? Memory? He couldn't keep his eyes in one place. They kept chasing motion—motion they couldn't quite catch. They were trying to watch the wind.

This is where I want to be, Henry thought. Why can't you be here, Henrietta? I'm sure you're someplace awful.

Henry turned and saw Richard's skinny legs kicking their way through the crack in the tree. Blake was already gone. He sighed again and dragged his toes as he walked.

CHAPTER TWELVE

Henrietta had hurried down the attic stairs but did not find her father on the landing. The light was not on beneath the bathroom door. Grandfather's door was still open, and its light was still on. Either her father had thumped in her parents' bedroom and not yet come out, had thumped in her parents' bedroom and wasn't coming out at all, or had already come out, seen the light on in Grandfather's bedroom, and gone in to look around for an explanation.

Henrietta ran on tiptoe across the landing to the partially open door. She looked through the crack and saw him step out of view. Her heart sank. She knew that her chances of ever being allowed to keep Grandfather's journals and key had just disappeared. But she was a bold girl, so she braced herself for the necessary conversation. Putting a smile on her face and squaring her shoulders, she stepped into the room.

She didn't say anything. Her mouth fell open, but not in any useful way. She was looking at the back of a small, old—if the white hair drifting out over his ears told the truth—mostly bald man. He was wearing the type of jacket she associated with old men. It was brown plaid and had badly sewn patches on the elbows. He was looking at the bookshelf, fiddling with the spines of the older-looking books, and muttering something under his breath.

There is no known protocol for how young girls ought to behave when discovering small older men puttering around in an already mysterious bedroom. Henrietta did her best.

"Excuse me," she said softly.

Knocking several books to the floor, the old man spun around. His face was small for his head, and he was holding one lens of a broken pair of glasses up to his left eye. He stared at Henrietta for a moment. She tried to smile. Then he dove to the floor more quickly than Henrietta would have thought possible. Henrietta started to ask him if he was all right, but he opened the cupboard door at the base of the bookshelf and began slithering in.

"Hey, wait," she said. "I just want to talk to you." She jumped over and grabbed his foot. He kicked her in the stomach, and she pulled his shoe off. She gulped air and sat down hard on the floor, watching the old man's feet disappear into the cupboard.

Henrietta hesitated. Another magic cupboard, and

in her grandfather's room. An old man. Her chance for answers had crawled away. Henrietta dropped to the floor and felt her way into the darkness. As her feet disappeared, Blake entered the room. He, more than Henrietta, was aware of the risks he took, though his cat-mind did not assess them. He ran straight into the cupboard at a speed only one of the local coyotes had seen and Dotty wouldn't have thought possible. He could see Henrietta's feet, and then he could not. The wooden back of the cupboard flicked into place, then disappeared again. Blake hit the darkness and felt the ground rise before emerging into long grass and sunshine. He did not need to look around to know that Henrietta was somewhere else. He turned and tried to push himself back down through the crack in the tree to the cupboard.

The way had shut behind him.

Blake was a wise cat, and he did not waste time worrying. He didn't know how. He walked to the stone, leapt onto it, and stretched out in the sun.

Henrietta froze. The music of violins, cellos, and a strange-sounding piano—like its strings were being plucked rather than hammered—came through the walls around her, filling the small, dark space where she crouched. And voices, laughing voices.

She was still in a cupboard, a cupboard wider and

deeper than Grandfather's. She sneezed. A cupboard
full of dust and cobwebs and, if she could believe her
hands, lots of dry mouse droppings. She pulled her
knees up under her, hunching over with her back
against the low ceiling, and felt around for the door.
Two feet in front of her and a little to one side, she
found it.

Henrietta only meant to open it a crack, but the
door swung open easily when she touched it and left
her blinking at all the light and the noise.

She looked out into an enormous ballroom with
black-beamed vaulted ceilings more than fifty feet
above a gleaming floor of inlaid wood. Huge paned
windows arched nearly to the ceiling between smooth
columns and bright frescoes. A small orchestra played
from a balcony at one end of the hall, and the floor
swirled with dancers. Full dresses of every one of the
world's colors spun on beautiful women no taller than
Henrietta. The hair on the women was piled high and
wrapped with strands of bright beads. The men all
wore their hair, which was almost universally black,
pulled tight and braided down their backs. They wore
trousers with wide legs down to the ankles and short
coats with sleeves that flared and stopped at the elbow.

Henrietta forgot the little man. She forgot Kansas.
She sat, unable to move, with her mouth open and her
eyes wide. She watched older men and women walk

alongside the walls, eating and laughing. She watched the musicians. She stared at the ceiling and floor, at the columns and windows and frescoes.

It was the most beautiful thing she had ever seen.

As her eyes ran over the dancers one more time, they stopped on one figure, a figure that she recognized. His back was to her, he was bald, and he was wearing a plaid jacket with big patches on the elbows. He was walking carefully through the dancers with only one shoe, watching his feet and setting each one down gently before he put his weight on it. None of the dancers seemed to notice him at all.

Henrietta pulled herself forward and stuck her head out the small door to see if anyone was near her. As she did, the color faded and the music stopped. The people disappeared. Only one figure remained, that of the strange old man in the jacket, picking his way carefully across a floor pocked with holes and rot.

Henrietta squeezed through the door, fell off a small ledge, and landed on the rough floor. Above her were the burnt and charred timbers of collapsed vaults, and a gray sky. The walls were black and gray with soot, the frescoes hidden, and the windows gaped shattered mouths.

"What happened?" Henrietta yelled. "Where did everything go?"

"Ha!" the little man laughed bitterly. Wood cracked beneath his foot and he pulled back.

Henrietta stood up to follow him. "Please tell me," she said. The floor was solid near the wall. She started walking carefully and quickly. It was like climbing through the lofts of some of the older barns, the ones that leaned sideways and were missing roofs or walls. "Tell me," she said again.

The little man turned around. "Look what you've done already—you've mussed everything. I'm no better off now than I was."

Henrietta stopped. "I didn't do this. I can't have. I just followed you."

The man glared at her. "If you mean destroying one of the world's great palaces, one of the world's great cities, then no. That was done by bigger fools than you. You made me lose my glasses."

"I'm sorry," Henrietta said. "I just wanted to talk to you. We could go back through and get them."

"Not likely," the man said. But he turned around and began walking back. "And you took my shoe."

"Well, you were trying to run off."

When the man reached her, he stopped and looked her up and down.

"I'm Henrietta," she said.

"I know." He walked past her, back toward the

cupboard, which was built into an enormous hutch, and he slid in with his legs sticking out. After a moment, he slid back out.

"Fate is no lady," the old man said. "It's closed right back up, and here we both are. You'll want to sit in that cupboard, never leave even for a moment, and wait for it to open. Likely take me a year, but now I'll be leaving to find what home I may still have." He bent over, took off his one shoe, and stuck it in his jacket pocket. He wasn't wearing any socks. Then he turned to walk off.

"Do you mean I'm stuck?" Henrietta asked. "Wait. Hold on. I want to talk to you."

The man faced her. "Are you going to pull on my leg?"

"Are you going to kick me?" she asked.

"What do you want to talk about?"

"Do you know how the cupboards work?"

The man shrugged. "Why do you need to know? Just fiddle about with them and see what happens. It will be good for everyone."

Henrietta took a deep breath, trying not to be annoyed. "Just tell me enough to get back when I need to."

"You'll not get back unless whoever's been spinning those knobs notices you're gone and is somehow able to locate where his norths were when you rode through on my feet. There's nothing you can do except spend your days leaning on the back of that cupboard, waiting. Oh, I've spent weeks doing just that in much nastier places, and the last few days as well—thanks to your meddling. When it opens, it won't be for long. You won't want to miss it. And get all your limbs through quickly. Now, I don't want to keep you. Goodbye."

Henrietta grabbed his coat and pulled him back. His caterpillar eyebrows came together, and he sputtered before he spoke.

"Never," he said, "have I encountered a small girl so inclined to grab an old man. Now, little girl, unhand."

"I'm as tall as you are," Henrietta said.

The old man's face turned red and his ears purple. He stepped toward Henrietta, looking straight into her eyes. She let go of his coat.

"Could you just tell me what happened to everything?" she asked. "What is this place? Where did everyone go?"

He rolled his eyes and shook his head.

"Don't you know?" Henrietta asked.

"Of course I know. It was a lifetime ago, but if you climb back in that hutch you can see me dancing, though I mostly ate sausages that night." He turned and pointed to the far end of the empty hall. "Over there. You wouldn't recognize me. I was a bit of a devil."

"A devil?"

"Apollonian. Handsome. Extremely good-looking."

Henrietta laughed. "What happened?"

"The stars fell, the moon went out, the earth shook— however you want to put it. Everything ended for the FitzFaeren in one night. But this hutch remembers. Wood remembers most things."

Henrietta looked back at the cupboard. "Where did all the people go?"

"Well," the little man said, "most died. I traveled and became a librarian."

"Why were you in my grandfather's room? What were you doing? My cousin saw you, didn't he?"

"Your cousin! The little weakling boy? Yes, he has eyes that can see. But I've had enough questions. The sun is setting, and I want to be far from this place before the light fades. In the dark, this place that was once alive tries to wake its memories. I have seen it try before, and I do not want to see it again."

"You mean it's haunted?" Henrietta asked. "I don't want to stay if it's haunted."

The man laughed. "If you ever want to see your home again, you will stay and wait. Do you have the second sight?"

Henrietta shook her head. "I don't know what you mean."

"Then it may not be as bad for you."

The little man moved down the long hutch, opening the larger doors until he found the one he wanted.

"What are you doing?" Henrietta asked.

"Leaving."

"How? Is that another magic cupboard?"

The man laughed and climbed through the small door, curling up to fit. "This is a dumbwaiter. From the middle of the room, I could see that the stairs have collapsed in the years since my last visit. Now goodbye to you and your questions."

Henrietta watched him pull a tight little rope from the back corner and then, accompanied by the high-pitched squealing of ancient pulleys, he descended out of view. She leaned in to watch him go, but he was already hidden from any light.

"You didn't tell me your name!" she yelled down the shaft.

"Ack! Don't shout! It's loud in here."

"What's your name?"

"Ask the sprites tonight." His voice rattled up at her through the shaft. He was almost down. Henrietta reached in and clenched the two little squealing ropes. They burned her hand, but they both stopped moving.

The old man's voice rose in anger. "Horrid little girl! Let go at once!"

Henrietta laughed and leaned back out of the echo. "Tell me your name."

She heard the man sigh. "Eli," he said.

"Eli what?"

"Eli FitzFaeren."

"Why were you in my grandfather's room?"

"I was living there."

"Why?"

"He was a friend. And a fool like his father before him and all his descendants. Now let go of the rope before I lay a curse on you."

"What really happened here?" Henrietta asked. "How did everyone die?"

Suddenly the rope glowed orange and went hot in her hand. She yelped and put her hand to her mouth. The pulley squealed as the rope rattled around it. Eli's yell poured out of the shaft as he fell. With a crack, the pulley ripped out of woodwork somewhere inside, and Henrietta watched it fall past the opening. The crash at the bottom filled the whole hall.

When everything was quiet, Henrietta stuck her head back in. She could hear groaning. "Are you okay?" she asked. The groaning turned into cursing.

"You!" the little man finally yelled. "You are as bad as your grandfather!" He went back to muttering.

"It was nice meeting you," Henrietta said.

Laughter echoed through the hall. "Surely you can't mean it. Enjoy your evening in the Lesser Hall of

FitzFaeren. Enjoy it, but do not eat anything, and more importantly, do not let anything eat you!"

Henrietta listened to him leave. When his footsteps and muttering had faded, she stood, chewing her lip, and turned to explore.

Richard and Blake sat on Henry's bed and looked around the attic room.

"This is where you live?" Richard asked. "It's filthy."

"I didn't like your room, either," Henry muttered. He was scanning Grandfather's journal and glancing up at the compass locks. "I don't know. There aren't really any more close combinations." He picked one, set the knobs, and sat down beside Richard. "This is the last one. If she's not here, then I'm waking up Uncle Frank."

Richard shrugged. "Fine," he said. "We can ask your uncle if I can stay."

"C'mon," Henry said, and the two of them snuck downstairs one last time.

Henry sat on the floor and stared at the cupboard. He was tired and he was nervous, and he was yawning again because he was both. He could die in one of these places. He shouldn't be doing this. Henrietta could die in one of them, too. He should wake up Uncle Frank.

"I will," he said out loud. "After this one. If I don't die. If *we* don't die."

"What?" Richard asked.

Henry didn't say anything. He was crawling through the cupboard. Richard watched.

Lying in bed, Frank told Dotty not to worry about the thumping or the trips on the stairs. Yes, he knew Henry was up, and probably the girls, too.

"The boy's white grass," he said. "Like when you leave a board in the yard. You pick it up after a coupla weeks or days even, and the grass underneath is all white and yellow. No sunshine. Only, Henry's been under a board in the yard for longer than a coupla days."

"The girls sound like they're up, too," Dotty said. "They're not getting any sleep."

"They'll recover," Frank said, and he slept.

When he woke, it wasn't because of any noise. He just felt a little funny. The sun wasn't up, but the sky was bright with the dawn. Dotty was asleep next to him.

Frank pulled himself out of bed and wandered, yawning, into the hall. He put his hand on the knob of the bathroom door and stopped. There was light coming into the hall from Grandfather's room. The door was partially open. Frank stared. He couldn't believe it. He stepped toward it, put out his hand, and pushed.

The door swung open easily. The curtains were open, and the room was light. There were flowers in a vase and some things on the floor, but Frank didn't notice. He was looking at the bed. A skinny boy with pants up to his ribs was sprawled on his back, asleep. He'd taken off some strange little boots, and his feet were bare. He had enormous chapped lips.

Frank walked to the bed and stood over the scrawny sleeper, examining his face. He coughed, and the boy's eyes popped wide open.

"Henry's in the cupboard," Richard said. "I opted to sit this one out. Would it be inconvenient for me to stay?"

CHAPTER THIRTEEN

Other men than Frank would have asked questions. They might have wondered who Richard was or why he was in the house. Frank walked to the cupboard, got down on his hands and knees, and eased himself in. Near the back, he stopped. There was a strange sucking sound accompanied by puffs of air. He let his eyes adjust to the dark cupboard and he stared, unblinking, at the back. It was flickering, sometimes there, sometimes not, dark with split seconds of light.

Frank backed out of the cupboard, stood, and left the room without even glancing at Richard. He went to the attic stairs and walked slowly up.

Henry's doors were open. He looked into the room. A blanket and a wad of taped-together posters were on the floor. There was no plaster on the wall, only cupboard doors, just how Frank remembered it.

Anastasia was on Henry's bed. She twisted around to look at Frank.

"Dad! Henry took the whole wall off, but look what he found. Have you seen these before? How do you open them?" She turned back around and spun one of the compass knobs. "I think you have to know the combinations."

"Don't touch those, Anastasia! Get off Henry's bed." Though she didn't hear it often, Anastasia recognized the tone in her father's voice. She let go of the knob and slid quickly off the bed.

"Where's Henry?" Frank asked.

"I don't know. We couldn't find Henrietta, either. They were both out of bed last night, but Penny wouldn't let me get up until it was light. She went to look for them in the barn. Who's he?" Anastasia pointed. Frank turned around and found Richard behind him, looking into the room.

"What's your name?" Frank asked.

"Richard Leeds," Richard said.

"Anastasia, I need you to concentrate," Frank said. "Do you remember what combination those knobs were set to before you touched them?"

Anastasia shook her head. "Did I do something wrong?" she asked. "What did I do?"

Frank smiled. "Go downstairs. Richard and I need to talk. Come tell me if you find Henry or Henrietta." Anastasia left for the stairs, and Frank put his hand on Richard's shoulder, pulling him into Henry's room.

Richard fidgeted nervously with his hands and then reached up to pull on his lip.

Frank was still in his pajamas, and his hair was standing out from his head. The two of them sat down on Henry's bed.

"What happened?" Frank asked.

"Henry crawled through a clock into my house, and I followed him back, but he didn't know. Then we looked for Henrietta and couldn't find her, though we found the cat. We went all sorts of places. Henry said he would attempt one more before waking Uncle Frank. I stayed back. Are you Uncle Frank?"

Frank nodded. He sat still for a moment and thought about what Richard had told him.

"Where do you live, Richard?"

"Hutchins," Richard said.

Frank's brow tightened. "Where's Hutchins?"

"It's in Britain," Richard said. "Are we in Britain?"

Frank shook his head. "No. We're in Kansas. What year is it in Hutchins?"

"Nineteen hundred eighty-nine. Queen Askew's reign."

"Wrong Britain." Frank drew in a long breath. "I figured it'd be somethin' like that. Are you tired, Richard?"

"Yes."

"You can sleep here for a while. I'll be back in a bit. I might have to wake you up."

Richard watched Frank leave and then flopped face down on Henry's bed. He was asleep before Frank reached the bottom of the stairs.

Dotty stood on the landing in her bathrobe. Her arms were crossed, her hair wandered, and her eyes were worried.

"What's going on, Frank?" she asked. "The room's open."

Frank stopped and took a deep breath. "Henry's gone through the cupboards. Henrietta's gone, too. She went first. He was looking for her."

Dotty leaned back against the wall and slid down until she was sitting on the floor. She put one hand over her mouth and then both over her eyes.

"I'm sorry, love," Frank said. "I should've stepped in. I just didn't want to fence him."

Dotty was very still.

"Dots, there's a boy upstairs that Henry brought back from one of the cupboards. He'll sleep for a while, but he's gonna need somethin' to eat."

Dotty stood up and looked in Frank's eyes. "Are you going after them?"

"I don't see much choice."

"Do you know which one they're in?"

"No. Anastasia was fiddlin' with the knobs when I went upstairs. I'll be guessin'. It might take a while."

Dotty clenched her jaw. "You belong here, Frank. You know that, don't you? Remember what I said."

Frank didn't say anything. Dotty turned and walked back into their room.

In Grandfather's room, Frank picked up the broken glasses and sat down on the floor. He pulled the rope out of the cupboard. The end was sliced cleanly. He stuck his arm into the small space and found a solid back. He thought for a moment and then went back up into Henry's attic. Richard was snoring.

Frank tried to look around quietly at first, but after a few loud creaks and crumpling posters, he realized Richard would be nearly impossible to wake. He bent down and examined the wall of cupboards, saw that the bed leg was wedged against the black one, and stood up.

Back downstairs, he found Dotty at the dining room table, still covering her mouth. She was not crying, and Frank knew that she wouldn't. Anastasia was standing in the corner of the room, leaning against the wall, watching. She had asked her mother what was wrong but hadn't been heard. Now she was waiting. Dotty looked up at Frank.

"Where is Henry?" Anastasia asked. "Is Henrietta with him?"

"Don't know," Frank said.

"Frank," Dotty asked, "do you think they'll be okay? I mean, really. Do you think you can even find them?"

Frank ran his hands through his hair and puffed his cheeks. "Honestly, Dots, I need to get lucky. I'm sure I can find them with enough time. It depends on how smart they're being, or who they've run into. Some places, that would be easy. Some places, that would be hard."

Frank sat down beside Dotty and set his fists on the table. "Anastasia," he said. "Run get your sister. Your mother's gonna explain things to you the best she can."

Anastasia just stood there.

"Go," Frank said. And she went. "Now," he said to Dotty, "I'm gonna start. Don't let the girls go upstairs unless you're with them. If you need to leave the house, that's fine."

"*You* should tell the girls."

"I don't have the time. Sooner I get started, the better." Frank kissed Dotty on the head and stood to go. He heard the back door burst open, and Penelope and Anastasia rushed into the room.

"I've got to go look for your sister and cousin," Frank said. "Your mother will try to explain things to you. When she's done, you make sure you do what she tells you." He turned and walked upstairs.

Penelope and Anastasia sat very still and looked at their mother. She looked at them.

"What are you going to tell us?" Penelope asked.

"I'm not sure," Dotty said.

"Where did Henry and Henrietta go?" Anastasia asked.

"I don't know. That's what your father is trying to figure out."

They were all silent. Finally, Dotty took a deep breath and spoke.

"Well, I suppose your father will be a while, so I may as well try to tell it." She reached up, pushed her hair behind her ears, and leaned onto the table. "I'll tell you as much as I know."

Both girls were listening, but Dotty stopped again. The girls held their breath, hoping she wouldn't change her mind. Then Dotty began in earnest.

CHAPTER FOURTEEN

"I was about your age, Penelope, walking home from school one day. It was the end of summertime, and school had just started. There were more people in Henry then, or it seemed like it, and they all loved baseball. There were lots of boys, and they had a system of teams picked, and each team had their own home field that they had claimed from some farmer. One of these fields used to be right out beside our house."

Dotty twisted and untwisted her fingers. She wasn't looking at her daughters. She was looking past years, sorting summers in her mind.

"On this day," she continued, "when I got home, my father was standing in the front yard watching a game, and there was a boy with him. I didn't want to have to meet the boy, so I snuck around to the back door and went inside.

"The boy was there for dinner, but he didn't talk to

me at all. He was older than I was, and he was lean and dark, with a bright smile and eyes that were always laughing. I'd never seen a boy sit up so straight or look right through you like he could, and he wasn't at all afraid of Daddy. Your aunt Ursula flirted with him the whole time. Mama and I didn't say much, and Daddy just kept telling us how well the boy could hit. He had a ring on his thumb, a big silver thing that people used to use to stamp wax—it had three starfish on it—and Ursula must have asked to see it at least a dozen times.

"The next day, when I was walking home, I saw the same boy playing in the park. I stopped to watch, and he really could hit. The day after that, I saw him at school. Everybody was talking about him—the grown-ups, too—but all the talk was about baseball and how he could help Henry High. An old couple, the Willises, let him move in with them."

"What?" Penelope asked. "Really? Is that why . . ."

Dotty smiled at her. "Just wait. I'm going too slow already. It was almost a year before I ever really did talk to him. I was walking home again, and he caught up to me. He said he needed my help to get back to his home. He was from a town in another place, where they didn't play baseball, and he needed to get back. He made me stop and sit down, and he told me a very strange story.

"The boys in his family were always sent off for a year to adventure before they could take their places in the town where he was from. Two of his brothers had gone to war and been killed. But his adventure had been different.

"My father had visited his town many times. He only went to their library, and at first, no one thought anything of it. But then some books, which were apparently important, began to disappear. Your grandfather was sent away, and the boy was sent to follow him.

"He followed my father all the way out of town and off the road, through hills and woods and finally into a hidden mountain valley. In the valley, swallowed by brush and vines, were the ruins of an old temple.

"The boy watched my father from a distance, watched him walk right up to a hole in the ruined wall and step through. He was gone. He waited for a while, but eventually the boy followed, and when he stepped through, something pushed him down onto his belly, and he crawled out into my parents' bedroom.

"He went straight outside as quickly as he could and ran into my father drinking lemonade on the front porch. My father recognized him, so the boy asked him if he was a sorcerer and whether he had stolen the books from the library. My father laughed and told him that he was just an explorer and took him out in the yard to show him baseball.

"His year of adventure turned into a year of baseball in Henry."

Anastasia couldn't wait for the end. "Grandfather was magic?" she asked. "For real?"

Dotty sighed. "No. He wasn't. But he'd found some. The boy told me that your grandfather could make a door in his bedroom lead to different places, and that he had to find a way to make it go back to his own town. Your grandfather told him that it wasn't possible anymore. The ruined wall had collapsed on the other side and the doorway had closed. The boy didn't believe my father, and he wanted me to help him.

"When my parents were out for dinner and Ursula was at a friend's, he came over and we went into the bedroom and looked at the cupboard. It didn't lead anywhere. So I took him up to my father's little office closet in the attic, where Henry has been living. The double doors were locked, and I watched while the boy kicked them open. Then we went into Daddy's closet and saw all the cupboards, along with books that your grandfather had taken. And there were some notes, naming the cupboards and explaining how the little doors worked. Any of them could be made to lead through the door in the downstairs bedroom."

Dotty stopped and looked at the wide eyes on her

daughters' faces. "The boy didn't recognize any of the names, so we went through and then came back and went through again. We did that until we went into a . . . very unfriendly place and someone tried to keep us. But your grandfather came, and managed to get us back through, and shut the cupboard behind us. He was very angry and told us that he was trying to find a way back and that he would help the boy when he did.

"Your grandfather never did. Or at least he said that he didn't. In the end, he stopped using the cupboards. Things had begun coming through them from the other side, both in the attic and in his room. Unpleasant things. One day, he just stopped locking the attic room, and when I looked in, all the cupboard doors were gone. He had covered them all with plaster.

"So the boy stayed in Henry awhile and kept playing baseball, because he couldn't ever go back."

Upstairs, Frank traded his pajama bottoms for old green pants with pockets on the legs that he had found at a yard sale. He opened the top drawer of an aged white dresser and dug his hands through the piles of mismatched striped tube socks before pulling out a sheathed knife. Frank slid the blade out of the sheath and watched it catch the light. It had been given to him when he was very young, and it was the only knife in the house that he had never sharpened. It was the reason why he sharpened everything else.

Frank tied the sheath to his belt, at the small of his back, and grabbed an old, sweat-lined blue baseball hat with a red *H* stitched to its front. Then he hurried out of the room.

On the landing, he dropped into a crouch, bouncing on his legs, then stood and twisted his torso back and forth, breathing deeply.

"Francis," a voice said behind him. "You've grown."

Frank spun in place. At the bottom of the attic stairs stood a woman, not tall but beautiful, holding a mangy cat. The cat looked at Frank, but the woman's pale eyes stared past him. She smiled, and her smooth olive skin glowed. Her hair, black as obsidian and straight, collected the light from the landing and shone as she moved.

"Where is the boy?" she asked. "Another sleeps in his bed." She stroked her cat. "And he had little strength to give."

Frank's throat tightened. He coughed. "What boy?"

The woman smiled and stepped toward him. Her voice was quiet, a cold breeze. "The boy who lives beside my cage. The boy who roused me from the maddening dark. The dream walker. The pauper-son. I have sampled his blood." Her eyes widened, looking through the walls around Frank. "Such blood!"

Frank's hand drifted toward his back.

"I could name his sires two centuries past. Fine bait you set for me, Francis, fifth of Amram's sons. A blood-vintage with strength enough, with life enough, to waken hope in a dried-up queen. Where is the boy?"

The woman stepped closer. Frank backed carefully across the landing toward Grandfather's room, gripping the knife handle behind him. He opened his mouth to yell, to warn his wife. No sound came. His tongue knotted, cramped, and tightened behind his teeth.

The soft chill of her voice washed over his face. "Your eyes betray you, Francis." She stood in front of him. "You would warn him? He cannot be far."

Frank struggled against the tangle in his tongue, against the numbness drifting through his limbs. He found an old strength.

Surging forward, Frank brought around his blade, a blade older than Kansas, older than the magic in the door behind him, as old as the evil he faced.

Words from another lifetime climbed up his throat and freed his tongue.

Dotty seemed almost surprised that she was done. She looked like she was still thinking.

"But I thought the boy was Dad," Penelope said. "Didn't you marry him? Why did you say he only stayed for a while?"

"What? Oh, yeah, I married the boy. He's your daddy. But he left Henry first. He went away to college in Cleveland and studied literature. After a year, I followed him."

"What happened?" Anastasia asked. "I didn't know Dad was the boy. Why didn't you just say that instead of calling him 'the boy' the whole time?"

Dotty shrugged. "I thought you'd figure it out," she said. "As for the rest, Henry uncovered the little cupboards in the attic, and he and Henrietta have gone through them. Your dad's looking for them."

"But does he know where they probably are?" Anastasia asked.

She didn't get an answer.

Old windows rattled with her father's voice. Above them, the ceiling shook.

CHAPTER FIFTEEN

Henry sneezed, waited, sneezed again, and squirmed closer to the mouth of whatever it was he was stuck in. At least there was light.

Someone was speaking. It was a man's voice, and he ended loudly. People applauded.

Henry got his face to the door as the music began and blinked in surprise. He saw what Henrietta had seen, though the dance and song had changed. His eyes followed the swirling colors, ran over the walls and up to the vaulted ceilings, where chains suspended three enormous gold candelabras lined with hundreds of flicking tongues of flame.

His eyes watered as another sneeze welled up in his head, and he buried his face in his arm to stifle the noise. Then he blinked and looked back into the sparkling hall.

"Who's there?" It was a girl's voice. In all the noise, he had barely even noticed it. Henry didn't say anything. He slid forward and stuck his head out into the room.

Instantly the world was black. He blinked again, waiting for his eyes to adjust. Some moonlight filtered down through the gapped roof, but no roof was visible. Henry scooted back into the cupboard. The laughter, the music, the light, and the noise of dancing feet all flooded back at once. He squinted and slid forward again, this time clipping his head on the top of the doorway. Darkness.

"Who's there?" the voice said again. This time it was the only noise in the room, and it ricocheted off the walls, filling the huge place.

"Henrietta?" Henry asked. "Is that you? Where are you?"

Henrietta laughed. "Henry? I'm way over here. The floor's all rotten, so I'm a little stuck now that it's dark. Do you have a flashlight?"

"Nope," Henry said. He slid all the way out and dropped to the floor. "Richard," he said back into the cupboard. "Richard? Come all the way through. What you're seeing isn't real."

Richard didn't say anything.

"Who is Richard?" Henrietta asked.

Henry didn't answer. "Richard? Richard? Oh well, it will be easier without you anyway."

Henry turned and looked around the ruined hall. He could see a few stars and the dim shapes of clouds, and he could make out the windows. "Where exactly are you?"

"I'm by the balcony."

"Where's the balcony? Are you by a window? I can only see windows."

"I'll try and come to you," Henrietta said. "Just keep making noise. I think I'll have to crawl."

Henry sat down with his back to the hutch. "You know you're a complete nut, don't you?"

"Takes one to know one," Henrietta said.

"Oh, shut up," Henry said. "Why would you go through a cupboard without telling anyone? I had no idea which one you went through."

The sound of cracking wood echoed around the hall, followed by clattering on the story below.

"Are you okay?" Henry asked. "Be careful."

"I'm fine," Henrietta said. "Close one, though. You were right. It wasn't a dream. There was this little man living in Grandfather's room. I was chasing him. If it helps, I'm glad you came. This place was getting spooky. Eli said it all got wiped out in one night, the night you can see from inside the cupboard, and now it's haunted."

"Who said?"

"Eli. The little man. Weren't you listening? He said this place gets freaky after dark."

Henry looked at the black shapes of the windows. "He was right."

"I'm standing up now," Henrietta said. "Can you see me?"

"No."

Light surged through the hall. Henry yelped and fell to his side.

"What's wrong?" Henrietta said. "Oops. I think I need to crawl again."

Henry sat up and shaded his eyes. The three huge candelabras that he'd seen lighting the dance were all suspended in the air, fully lit. The room was still in complete decay. There wasn't even any ceiling left to hold two of the three lights. Henrietta was near the end of the room on her hands and knees. She stuck out one hand and felt around the floor for holes, then slid forward carefully and did it again.

"Henrietta?" Henry asked.

"Yeah?"

"Can you see?"

She laughed. "I thought my eyes would get used to it, but they didn't. This is crazy dark."

"I can see you," Henry said. "I can see everything. The big chandelier lights are on."

Henrietta stopped. She was only about sixty feet

from Henry. Her eyes were wide and she turned her head, staring blankly around her.

"I'm going to come get you," Henry said. He stood up and looked over the floor. The larger pits were all near the center of the room, but the distance between where he stood and where Henrietta crawled was littered with smaller gaps and cracks.

Henry walked cautiously around the split and sagging wood, trying to keep above beams and supports. Henrietta kept crawling.

"Stop," Henry said. "Just wait. I'm halfway there."

Six feet from her, he stepped over the last gap and touched her on the back. She stood, groping blindly for his hands.

"Okay, I can kind of see you now," she said. "At least, I can see your shape."

Henry looked around for an easier way back. Then he heard something, a few notes from a violin. A burst of laughter. Something swished behind him.

Henry spun, almost knocking Henrietta over, just in time to watch a dark woman, shorter than he was and wearing a fire-orange gown, swirl past him, arms out, embracing an invisible partner. Her eyes were shut and she was laughing.

More and more people appeared, usually dancing alone, occasionally in pairs. The music came rarely and in short bursts. The people danced regardless, breaking the silence of the hall with the rustling of fabric.

"What's going on?" Henrietta asked. "I thought I heard something."

"The people are dancing," Henry whispered. He shivered. "C'mon. I want to get out of here."

"I feel sorry for them," Henrietta said.

Henry tried to keep his eyes on the dancers and on the floor. Once or twice he collided with one. He had expected to wisp right through him, but he didn't. He felt the bump, though lightly, and then the dancer, or dancers, would spin away. One even said, "Pardon."

Henrietta saw none of it. She clung to Henry's arm and placed her feet nervously wherever Henry told her the floor was strong. When only a third of the distance to the cupboard remained, the ballroom was nearly full, and collisions were almost impossible to avoid. Henry kept his arms out, and the dancers spun off to the sides as they came.

"Is that wind?" Henrietta asked.

"Yes," Henry said. "The air is moving."

He was guiding Henrietta in front of him when the two doors at the end of the hall burst open.

Henrietta grabbed at him. "What was that?" she whispered. "What do you see?"

Henry didn't say anything. He and most of the

dancers were frozen, staring at the doorway. Through it stepped a tall figure hooded and cloaked in wolf skin, holding a slender staff taller than he was. At the top, a long, narrow spike rose out of two cruel blades that bent back toward the shaft. Broad men, none as tall as the first, swarmed into the room.

Then the screaming began. Henrietta could hear it. She dropped out of Henry's grip and covered her ears. Henry stood and watched, and felt that familiar sickness welling in his stomach. Some of the men held lean wolves on chains, and when the tall man gestured, they released them, snarling, into the crowd.

The wolves attacked a few, but mostly they herded the dancers to the center of the room. A few still danced alone, and the wolves either did not see them or were unable to touch them. As the people gathered, Henry pulled Henrietta to her feet. Whatever was going to happen next, he didn't want to see it. The hall was filled with screams and weeping, and Henry did not turn around. Henrietta cried while Henry shuffled her toward the wall with the hutch, and as he watched his feet and the floor around them, he saw a man running from a wolf. He was tall, not one of the short people, and he was running toward the hutch. He looked over his shoulder, and Henry blinked. The man had his mother's face. He threw open the cupboard, and the wolf snapped at his feet as he dove inside.

When he was gone, the wolf turned, still snarling, and surveyed the room. It looked directly at Henry, raised its hackles, and pulled its lips back.

"Silence!" The tall man's voice rose above the din. The broad men all began whistling, and wolves from every corner of the room returned to them. The wolf in front of Henry ran to its handler, guarding the perimeter of what was now a crowd of several hundred gathered on the dance floor. One of the small men broke away from the group and ran for the doors. Two wolves pulled him down from behind, and the screaming began again.

"Silence!" The man's voice was thunder. This time he gestured with his staff, and the great windows exploded into shards, showering the crowd with glass. "You have long kept out the Witch-Queen with your tokens! Nimiane now sees that your tokens are gone, and so will you be. We are the Witch-Dogs, and she feeds us well."

Henry tried not to listen. He tried not to watch. He pushed and dragged Henrietta to the wall and then shoved her into the cupboard.

"Hurry!" he said. He had to yell as the noise mounted again. "Close your eyes and push through!"

Henrietta crawled in, but her feet never disappeared. "It won't open for me!" she shouted back at him.

Henry burrowed in next to her. "Okay, scoot to the side as much as you can. When I'm most of the way through, grab onto my legs and crawl after me with your eyes shut."

Henry levered himself up, gripped the rope, and tried to pull himself forward. The rope slid toward him. The end was cut cleanly.

The two of them lay in the cupboard while wolves howled and glass shattered, while people screamed and men laughed. In the end, the voices were silent. The ceiling crashed and the timbers burned.

Dotty jumped up from her chair and ran to the stairs. Penelope and Anastasia followed her up.

On the landing, she slowed and looked around. Grandfather's room was still open, but nothing seemed wrong. She looked back and saw both girls behind her holding their breath.

"You two *stay*," she whispered.

She walked softly across the landing and came to Grandfather's halfway-open door. She saw Blake, and then she saw Frank's feet. He was lying flat on his back. She stepped closer and pushed on the door. It swung slowly, and she saw Frank's legs, his waist, his chest, his face. His eyes were shut. One arm lay flat, the other was bent, the hand clutching something above his hip. It was his knife. The blade was smeared red.

With a gasp, Dotty threw the door open and rushed to him. Dropping to her knees, she grabbed at his throat, feeling for a pulse.

"Dorothy," a voice said.

Dotty spun and went white when she saw the speaker. The witch was fingering her cat and staring above Dotty's head. She was smiling

"Mom?" Anastasia's voiced drifted in the door.

"Shhh," Penelope said.

Dotty tried to yell, to tell them to run. Her tongue was frozen.

The witch laughed. "They can't hear you." Her laughter grew, and then broke. She coughed. With each hack her image changed, and Dotty glimpsed what she already knew was there—the shriveled form of a tiny eyeless hag. Dotty lunged for her feet but landed heavily on the floor. She tried to stand, but a smell like foul eggs surrounded her and she couldn't breathe. She half stood, dizzy, and her knees gave. Her elbows went limp. "Run," she whispered.

Anastasia and Penelope had seen their mother hurry into Grandfather's room. All they'd heard was laughter, then coughing.

"Mom?" Anastasia said again. Penelope bit her lip.

A woman like they had never seen emerged from the doorway, smiling sadly and carrying a cat. Both girls stepped back, and Anastasia grabbed Penelope's arm. The woman was dressed heavily, as if for the cold, with a gray cloak. But her throat was bare. It was a long throat, and delicate. The face above it was just as rich as it was fine, the olive skin as smooth as it was warm. She was beautiful. Her cheeks were high and her nose long, how Anastasia thought a queen's should be. A queen in any land, in any country.

"Children," she said softly. "Your father has been winded, but your mother is tending him."

Penelope swallowed loudly. "Who are you?"

"I am called Nimiane. I am a friend of your father's from another place. He has asked me for my help. It is important. There was a boy. Do you know where he is?"

"Henry?" Anastasia asked. "He's lost in the cupboards."

"Can we see our parents?" Penelope asked.

"Soon enough," Nimiane said. "Show me these cupboards. Are they the small gateways in the room above?"

"Mom?" Penelope called. "Can we come in?"

"Hush. Hush," Nimiane said. "We must leave them

for a few moments." She tried to look at Penelope's face but missed, looking just above her head.

"Your cat looks sick," Anastasia said.

The woman turned her face toward Anastasia. "Yes. He has been sick for some time, but I am able to keep him alive."

Anastasia stared into the cat's eyes. Then she looked up at the woman's perfect face. "What's wrong with your eyes?" she asked. "Why don't you look at us?"

"My eyes are strong," Nimiane said, her tone suddenly harsh. It softened quickly. "I have a little magic, and I do not always need to look in order to see. Now, will you take me to these cupboards? I would ask you about them."

Anastasia stepped to the attic stairs, but Penelope didn't budge. "We'll stay down here," she said.

"Your father asked that we hurry," the woman said. "This boy Henry is not in a pleasant place."

"C'mon," Anastasia said. "We'll come back in a second."

"Mom?" Penelope said. "We're going into the attic. We'll be right back."

Anastasia stood at the top of the stairs and waited. Nimiane waited for Penelope to climb first. When Nimiane did move onto the stairs, she held the cat low, and her steps were not smooth.

In the attic, Anastasia pulled the two doors open and stepped into Henry's room. "Oh, I forgot about Richard," she said. "He's still asleep."

The witch walked into the room behind her.

"Who's Richard?" Penelope hung back, but then she saw Richard's face. His flesh was gray. A purple blotch stood out on his forehead. "He doesn't look asleep," she said. "Is he okay?" She slid past the woman's robes and put her hand on his cheek. "He's cold."

"His sleep is merely deep," the woman said.

Penelope put her fingers against Richard's neck. "His heart is barely beating."

Nimiane raised her head and sniffed. "These are all the gateways?"

"What about Richard?" Anastasia asked.

The woman turned on her sharply, then slowed herself and smiled. She stretched out a slender arm to touch Richard.

"There it is," Penelope said. "It's beating faster now."

Nimiane turned back to the cupboards. "These— cupboards. How are they used?"

"I thought you were from one," Anastasia said.

"Yes," the woman said. "I found the way in. It was very small, but I passed into the darkness to question some of the eldest, and it was my own father who told me how to pass through the small ways. So I have come and so I will go. But the boy Henry must have another way. He could not know such magic."

"We don't know how it works," Penelope said. "We've never done it. Mom just told us that Henry and Henrietta were stuck in them."

"I think you spin the knobs on the middle one," Anastasia began. Penelope shot up her eyebrows behind the witch's back and shook her head. Anastasia stopped. Penelope was backing slowly toward the door.

"Go on," the witch said.

"That's it." Anastasia shrugged. "I think you spin the middle ones."

Nimiane shifted her cat, lifting it higher, and then stretched out a hand, running it over the doors. "Childish," she said. "So clumsy. You are behind one of these, young pauper-son? The blood of Mordecai, hidden in a cupboard?" She raised her hand and spoke a strange, rough word. The doors all flew open, and Anastasia's ears popped.

Penelope grabbed Anastasia by the wrist and dragged her out of the room. They reached the top of the stairs too quickly and slid most of the way down on their backs.

"Children!" the woman cried, but they hit the landing, staggering into a run. The black cat dashed between them.

"Mom!" Penelope yelled. "Mom!"

The two of them burst into Grandfather's room, the cat with them. Anastasia ran into the bed while Penelope slid to the floor.

Blake rose from where he had been sitting by Dotty's head and charged the sickly cat, yowling. Dotty lay crumpled on her side next to Frank. Her skin was pale and her lips were blue.

"Mom?" Anastasia said. "Penelope! Are they dead?"

The black cat retreated to the landing and Blake followed. Penelope crawled to her parents. She didn't answer. The two sisters could hear footsteps on the attic stairs.

Anastasia rushed to the door. "She's coming, Penelope!"

"Shut it," Penelope said, but Anastasia didn't. "Shut it!" she said again.

"Blake! Come here!" Anastasia turned and grabbed Blake by the loose skin on his neck, hurried into the room, and shut the door behind her. Then she stuck her finger in the doorknob hole and pulled. The door wouldn't open.

Penelope pressed fingers into her mother's neck. After a moment, she moved to her father. "They're alive," she said. "Can you hear anything?"

Anastasia stuck her ear to the door. Penelope rolled Dotty onto her back and brushed her mother's hair out of her face. Dotty's eyes were open, but her pupils were no more than tiny points.

"No," Anastasia whispered. "I can't." Then she jumped back, tripped on Frank's foot, and fell on the floor.

The door rattled in its frame.

CHAPTER SIXTEEN

Zeke was walking. He had his glove on his head, and he was holding a wooden bat in his left hand. In his right, he tossed a baseball. He would drop it onto the bat, let it bounce, and catch it. Then he would drop it, bounce it twice on the bat, and catch it. Then he would drop it, bounce it as many times on the bat as he could, and lunge for it when it hopped off to the side. His record was thirteen while walking, twenty-two stationary. He was walking to Frank and Dotty's house to find Henry. It was early, but he wanted to hit for a while and still have time to take Henry outside of town to the abandoned Smythe farm. Before the daily game started, he wanted to show him the old car in the horse stall and the rusted-out tools in the loft.

When he reached the steps to the front porch, he stopped. Twelve, thirteen, fourteen, fifteen, and the ball skipped off the side of his bat into the grass. He bent over, picked it up, and continued on to the porch. He could hear the phone ringing inside. He opened the screen door and knocked. Then he opened the front door.

"Henry? Mrs. Willis, is Henry here?" The phone kept ringing. Zeke stepped into the house and looked around.

"Mrs. Willis?" he yelled again. A black cat ran down the stairs in front of him and stopped about three steps up. It sat, and stared. Zeke yelled again, this time louder.

"Mrs. Willis?" The phone stopped ringing, and he heard something upstairs. He stepped onto the bottom stair and listened. The cat didn't move.

"What?" he shouted. He thought he could hear one of the girls yell something back. He'd better wait a minute. He didn't just want to walk right up. He reached down to scratch the cat's ear, but there was a large bald spot, an oozing sore on its back that wrapped down around its side and chest. He didn't know how he'd missed it. The cat didn't have a collar.

"I don't think you're supposed to be in here," he said. "Mrs. Willis would probably take you to the vet if we had one, but I'm not as nice." The cat opened its mouth and hissed at him. Zeke stepped back, then he held his bat out over the cat and tapped it on the back.

"C'mon," he said, and tapped it again. The cat turned and tried to run up the stairs, but Zeke flipped it onto its side and dragged it writhing down the stairs with the bat on its belly. At the bottom, it flipped quickly back onto its feet and tried to bolt around him. Zeke kicked it, herding the cat with the bat and his feet toward the front door. He leaned over, pushed the screen door open, and tossed the cat onto the porch with his foot. He let go of the screen door, and it slam-rattled shut as the cat collected itself and jumped back toward the house. .

Zeke expected the cat to run away, but it stood on its hind legs, clawing at the screen and staring at him with angry eyes. Zeke rubbed the scratches on his calf and shin, then turned to look back into the house.

"Hello?" he yelled up the stairs. "Can I come up? Is Henry here?" This time he heard a voice from somewhere, muffled but much clearer.

"Don't come up!"

"Is that you, Penny?" he asked, but the phone started ringing again. "I'll wait," he added, and then sat on the bottom step, listening to the phone. But he wasn't patient. When the ringing stopped, he stood again and looked up the stairs.

"I'm coming up!" he yelled. "Just through to Henry's room!"

"Don't!" It was Anastasia.

"Why not? Is Henry here?"

"No, he's not!" It was Penelope's voice.

"Anastasia?"

"Yeah?"

"Where's your mom?"

"She's up here, too."

"Are you okay?"

Anastasia didn't answer. Neither did Penelope. Then one of them screamed.

Zeke ran upstairs.

Penelope and Anastasia sat on the floor by their parents. Dotty's breath was rattling in her throat. Frank breathed easily, but a pool of blood grew in the carpet at his side. The door boomed and rattled again.

"You are young to know how to shut a door so well. Has someone shut it for you?"

Anastasia crept to the door, put her eye to the small hole, and looked out, directly into the eyes of the black cat. The woman was holding the cat to the door. She laughed. Then she coughed, and it didn't seem that she would be able to stop. But she did, and when she did, she spoke again.

"Your blood is familiar to me, but it is not strong enough for this magic. I have met your sister, and she was weak. She is with the boy Henry?"

Anastasia opened her mouth to answer, but Penelope poked her and put her finger to her lips.

"You do not need to answer me," the witch said. Her voice was harsh. All sweetness was gone. "Henry's blood is stronger. Just a little of his life has given me much."

The door rattled again. Plaster on the wall cracked. "And I've known your mother. I met her before she grew old and fat. Her weak blood runs in your veins. Francis was bolder. We will see if she wakes or if the sleep keeps her. I remember your grandsire, though the earth now chains him. I even knew your mother's grandsire for a little while. It has been long since your family disturbed my mother's rest in the cold darkness, but it is always your family.

"I thought the way had been lost, but disturbance came again. Where is the boy Henry that pricked me? I do not smell him." She grew silent. The girls could hear the phone ringing downstairs.

Anastasia put her eye back to the door and saw the woman bend down and place the cat on the floor. The cat, crouching, hurried down the stairs.

"She doesn't know what the phone is," Anastasia whispered to Penelope. "She sent the cat downstairs to find out."

Then the woman coughed, and Anastasia saw her face.

She had no eyes. Where her eyes ought to have been were swollen sores, red against her white skin. Around the sores were the trailing scratches of fingernails. Her head was shorn near-bald, but the stubble of her hair was dark.

Anastasia heard the front door open and the screen door slam. Someone was yelling.

"It's Zeke," Penelope whispered. "He shouldn't come up. She'll gas him to sleep or something."

"Penny," Anastasia said. "She doesn't have any eyes. She must be blind. Is that why she can smell us?"

"Don't come up!" Penelope yelled. Then the two of them sat and listened. They could hear Zeke yelling for their mother.

"He didn't hear you."

"Don't come!" Penelope yelled. "Up!" she added. They both listened.

"The phone stopped ringing," Anastasia said. "Do you think he answered it?"

"Zeke wouldn't answer somebody else's phone. I hope he leaves."

"Penny, do you think she was lying about Mom maybe not waking up?"

They both looked at Dotty, breathing slowly on her back. Blake was lying on her stomach.

"I think Mom will be fine. I don't know about Dad. There's a lot of blood—coming from his mouth, too—and I don't know what to do."

They heard Zeke again. The cat was hissing somewhere. Blake walked to the door, and Anastasia stood up and stuck her ear against it. She pulled back quickly.

"The door's hot," she whispered, and she ducked down to peer through the hole again. This time she couldn't see through it. It had been plugged.

"What is Zeke doing downstairs? He really should go." Penelope yelled again while Anastasia looked for something to poke through the hole. The screen door slammed downstairs. The phone was ringing again.

"Penny, I think she's trying to burn the door down."

"Don't come up!" Penelope yelled.

"Stop worrying about Zeke," Anastasia said. "We have to figure out what we're going to do."

"I don't want him to get hurt."

"Because you like him," Anastasia muttered.

Penelope wheeled on her. "Everybody likes him, and even if I didn't, I wouldn't want a witch to gas him."

"Because you love him."

"Stop it, Anastasia!" Penelope's voice hardened. "This is not the time."

Anastasia sniffed. "We have to figure out what we're going to do if the witch gets the door open."

"Well, there's nothing really that we can do," Penelope said. "She won't get it open. Dad never could."

Anastasia dug her little finger into the keyhole. "Dad isn't a witch."

"Yeah," Penelope said. "But he used a chain saw."

"I'm coming up! Just through to Henry's room!" Zeke's voice was loud and clear.

"Don't!" Anastasia yelled.

"Why not? Is Henry here?"

"No, he's not!" Penelope yelled.

"Anastasia?"

"Yeah?"

"Where's your mom?"

"She's up here, too," she said.

"Are you okay?" Zeke shouted.

The girls heard a scraping behind them, and Blake jumped off Dotty. One of the windows was open a crack, and the black cat was squirming through it. Penelope screamed, and Anastasia ran to the window and pushed it down. The cat's howl mixed with Penelope's while Anastasia pushed the window back up and tried to shove the cat's head out. It bit her hard on the hand and dug its front claws into her wrist and pulled itself in. She shook her arm out the window, but the cat was wrapped around it. Then Blake was wrapped around it as well.

Anastasia jumped up and down beside the window, jerking her arm as the catfight climbed around it. The two cats flew off and out the window and rolled down the roof over the front porch. Anastasia looked at her bleeding arm, then watched as Blake broke free and ran back toward her. When he was in, she slammed the window hard, sat down on the bed, and tried not to cry. Blake was already relaxed, licking his own slight wounds next to her. The black cat pressed its face on the glass of the window, turned, and left.

"Who are you?" Zeke asked. The woman stood on the landing and smiled at him. Her hair was long and black and seemed to be catching all of the light on the landing. Her pale eyes were the loveliest gray, or green, or blue, that he had ever seen. But there was something strange about them.

"I'm the girls' godmother," she said. Her voice was lovely. He wanted her to talk more. "I'm staying for a little while." Zeke stepped up one more stair, but her eyes didn't follow him. Not at first.

"Why didn't you say anything? I was yelling."

"Were you?"

"Yeah." Zeke stared at her. She was perfect, but he didn't think he would like it if she tried to touch him. "Is Henry here?" he asked. "I heard the girls screaming, so I came up. Why didn't they want me to?"

"Oh, they were being bathed and the cat startled them."

This made no sense at all to Zeke, but he didn't argue. "Is Henry here?" he asked again.

"I wonder? I was looking for him myself. I have something for him. Come here, and I will give it to you. You may pass it on when you find him."

"Zeke?" Penelope's voice came through the door. "Are you okay?"

"Yeah, I'm fine," Zeke said.

"Is the witch gone?" Anastasia asked. Zeke looked at the mutilated door to Grandfather's room and then back to the beautiful woman. She was still smiling.

"Your godmother's out here."

"What?" both girls said.

"Your godmother."

"She is not!" Anastasia yelled. "Run, Zeke, quick! She's a witch, and she's already gassed Mom and Richard, and Dad's hurt!"

Zeke stepped back down another stair. Again, the woman didn't notice. She turned from the bedroom door and smiled toward where Zeke had been standing.

"We've been at all sorts of games today," she said, and then she started laughing. Her laugh was extraordinarily pleasant. Zeke couldn't leave. But then she coughed, and his stomach tightened. She coughed again, and this time he saw clearly. The woman's hair was gone, and he didn't know what had happened to her eyes. But it was only a moment. She was laughing again, and beautiful. He stepped quickly up the rest of the stairs and onto the landing. He put his back to the wall across from her, next to the attic stairs, and watched, trying not to breathe. He was gripping his bat. The woman smiled even more broadly, put a finger to her lips, and looked where Zeke had just been standing.

"Do you know—" she began in a whisper, but stopped. Her nostrils flared only slightly, and then she turned her head slowly, faced Zeke, and poured her smile out on a spot on the wall just beside his head.

"Do you know of any other way into the room?" she whispered. "They have locked me out, and if I do not find a way to catch them, then I have to mix them a lamb pudding. Perhaps Henry could help? We could go find him together." She took a careful step toward Zeke, and then another. He slid slightly to the left. He saw her nose twitch, and she adjusted her course. Then he slid back, and one step later, she followed him. She was too close to him already, but he waited.

"Some openings," she said, still smiling, "require boy's blood." Her hand, holding a small knife, flicked out toward him. He hopped up onto the attic stairs and jumped down behind her. He bumped into her as he jumped, and her arm swung out and around, but too slowly. She no longer tried to hide her flaring nostrils as she spun around, sniffing until she faced him.

"Wretch," she said. "Torturing my cat—my eyes. One sliced finger is all I need, but I'll slice more than that. I'll store you deep in the darkness, where they only feed on faeries. You'll be left alive enough to feel it."

Zeke was still backing up in front of her. He had both hands on the bat, and this time he was going to swing. But she stopped.

"Faeries?" she said to herself. "Faeries?" She laughed. "My mind has been too long wandering if I have missed a closing spell of the faeren." She turned from Zeke and stepped toward Grandfather's door.

Henry opened his eyes and spat out Henrietta's hair. Air was moving on his face. That hadn't happened since the two of them had crawled into the cupboard. Henrietta, still sleeping, shifted beside him. It was less dark than it had been, but it still wasn't light. He was extremely stiff. He levered himself up onto one elbow and twisted to look down past his curled body.

His feet were near the open side of the cupboard door. Through it, he saw the ruined hall, empty, decayed, and lit by daylight. But that's not where he had felt the air. The air had been on his head, in the dark end of the cupboard.

Henry twisted back and put out his hand. It disappeared in front of him. He twiddled his fingers around and felt the air. It was cooler than the air in the cupboard. He slid forward and Henrietta groaned. The cupboard was open, but not into Grandfather's room. The opening was barely big enough for his head.

Henrietta kicked him in her sleep. He kicked back and pushed himself forward as hard as he could. His forehead and eyes emerged into light. His shoulders banged against something and would go no farther.

Henry blinked and tried to turn his head. The space was narrow, but he managed to move a little, enough to recognize his bed. His head was sticking through the wall into his bedroom, and he was looking down at Richard.

"Hey," Henry said. "Richard. Wake up, you little moron."

Richard didn't move, so Henry pulled in a deep breath, preparing to shake the house down with his yelling. He blew it right back out. All the cupboard doors he could see were open. All of them. He couldn't see the doors down by the floor, but he felt something in his stomach.

Endor was open.

He looked back at Richard. Something was wrong. Henry could see him breathing, but his skin was gray.

"Richard!" he said quietly. "Richard, wake up. Richard. Annabee is coming! Quick! Wake up!"

Richard moved one hand.

"Richard!" Henry was worried as well as claustrophobic. He gathered all the moisture in his mouth, tipped his head, and spat.

Most of it landed on the bed, but the spray caught Richard's chin. Henry ran his tongue around the inside of his cheeks, gathered more saliva, and tried again. The spit landed on Richard's forehead.

Henry waited, holding his breath. Richard shifted slightly and began snoring. Henry didn't have much more moisture to work with. His tongue gathered and he let it pool in his jaw. When he had enough, he spat.

He was disappointed. It didn't stay together. But it all hit Richard in the face.

"Richard!" Henry said. "Come on, please!"

Richard's eyes opened and looked directly into Henry's. "I feel ill," he said.

"Well, get me out of here, and I'll find you some medicine."

"Why is my face wet?"

"I don't know. Just stand up and help me out of here."

"What are you doing?" Richard sighed and shut his eyes.

"No, Richard! Up! Up! I found Henrietta."

Richard rolled over and sat up on the end of the bed. "What would you like me to do?"

"Set the combination back to this cupboard. Then we can come out downstairs."

"I don't know the combination."

"You were with me when I set it! Wait a second. Do not lie back down! I'll get it out of my backpack."

Henry slid all the way back into the hall and glanced around. Then he pulled out Grandfather's journal and scanned the list until he recognized the combination.

Henrietta woke up. "What are you doing?"

"Getting us out of here. Hold on. Hop out so I can get all the way in."

Henrietta did, and she groaned while she stretched. Henry climbed back inside. "Up, Richard, up!" she heard him say. "Okay, here it is. No. Don't do it yet. It might cut my head off."

Henry slid out again, next to Henrietta, and smiled. "We're going," he said. Henrietta was staring at the ceiling. He glanced up. "I don't ever want to see this place again." Henrietta didn't say anything.

Henry climbed in first. Henrietta followed on his heels.

* * *

The witch ran her hands across the door's surface and around the frame. Zeke stepped toward the stairs. She sniffed at him but kept her hands on the wood.

"You have the faeren shut your doors! A strength so far beneath me I almost overlooked it." She stepped back and stretched both hands in front of her.

One word rumbled slowly in her throat and the door flew open, knocking Anastasia over onto her father. Penelope's mouth opened, but she could not scream.

Henry crawled into the room and froze, unable to take in the scene all at once. The witch stepped into the doorway and took a deep breath.

"The boy Henry," she said, sniffing. She smiled. "Your blood will run stronger in my veins."

Henrietta pushed Henry from behind and came out beside him.

"Mom?" She ignored the witch and crawled straight to her mother's body. Then she saw her father. "Is he dead?" she cried. "Penelope, is he dead?"

She didn't wait for an answer. She stood up and ran straight at the witch, throwing herself at the woman. The witch lurched back and gasped as Henrietta's shoulder drove into her stomach. Henry took two steps and lunged at the woman, hitting Henrietta in the shoulder blades and the witch in the ribs. The three of them teetered in the doorway.

Henry banged his head against her as hard as he could and swung drunkenly with his fists. He felt two inhuman hands close on his throat. A throbbing pulse surged into him, and in one blinding moment, his skull crackled and his body and mind went limp.

Penelope and Anastasia saw the witch step back and catch her heel in the carpet nest created by the chain saw. She fell, and Henry and Henrietta fell with her.

The bat was already off Zeke's shoulder. His knees were bent. Hips rotated. Arms extended. The ash shaft swung as fast as it ever had in the fields. Before the three bodies bounced on the floor, Zeke's bat whistled through Henry's hair and smacked into the witch's temple.

The house was still. Henrietta struggled to pull herself out from under Henry. She stood up shaking, tears still running down her cheeks.

"Henry?" Zeke said. He threw his bat down. The end was smoking. "Henry!"

The witch lay still, now visible for what she was—a shriveled body, eyeless and bald. Henry lay on top of her, head to head, cheek to cheek. Zeke grabbed Henry's body, pulled him off, and laid him on his back in the bedroom. A splatter of the witch's blood was steaming on his jaw.

"He's breathing," Zeke said.

Something crashed down the attic stairs and tumbled onto the landing. Zeke spun and grabbed for his bat.

"Who's that?" he asked.

"Richard," Anastasia said. "He fell down the stairs."

Outside, the black cat, which had been scratching at the mudroom door, relaxed. Cats do not yearn for freedom. Most of them just have it—even when they are pampered, owned, and cared for. This cat did not know that it had been a slave. It did know that it needed a drink. And it could smell mice in the barn and peeper frogs in the tall grass beyond it. It did not know that it had been possessed. It did not know that the inside of its head had never been its own, that there was a woman who had seen the world through its eyes. The cat, which had no name, knew none of this. But something had changed. If it had known what, it would have run as far away as possible, run until collapse. Instead, it turned around slowly, stretched its paws as far as they would reach, straightened the kinks out of its back, and walked off into the grass to find a drink and a place to lie down.

"What are we going to do now?" Anastasia asked.

"We have to call the sheriff," Penelope said.

"Not with her here," said Henrietta. "We can't explain her."

"I don't even know what's going on," Zeke said. "She tried to stab me. She's really a witch, isn't she?"

"Well, she's dead now," Penelope said.

"No, she's not," Zeke said. "She should be, but I just knocked her out. She's still breathing." All three of them looked at the body, face up on the floor. The chest, under the gray cloak, was rising and falling slowly.

"We should kill her," Anastasia said.

"What? We can't do that!" Penelope was shocked. "Anastasia, that's awful. We can't just kill someone who's unconscious. What would you do, anyway?"

"Well, she's got a knife, and she stabbed Dad, and she tried to stab Zeke. We should just stab her in the neck or something."

"We can't kill her," Penelope said. "Zeke, tell Anastasia how awful that would be."

Zeke looked around at the bodies on the floor. "Well, I don't know what all is going on. But we do need an ambulance now."

Frank and Dotty lay side by side. Zeke moved Henry beside Frank and carried a moaning, delirious Richard in and set him beside Dotty. He'd broken his wrist.

"The witch is going to wake back up," Zeke said.

"I would like taffeta," Richard muttered. "Yellow."

Anastasia sniffed loudly. "You don't have to watch, Penny. I can stab her."

"No, and you wouldn't even know how," Penelope said. "Anastasia, go call now. Tell them that there have been some accidents, and a man has been stabbed."

Anastasia stood up and walked toward the stairs. "I'd just stick it in her neck. She's going to wake up, and when she does, there's nothing we can do to her."

Penelope ignored her. "We could lock her in the basement," she suggested.

Henrietta had been sitting silently beside her mother. "Stick her through a cupboard," she said quietly.

Penelope looked at her. "I don't think we should do that," she said. "We don't know where we'd be sending her. Some poor people might just have a witch all of a sudden."

"Well, I think it's either that or let Anastasia stab her in the neck," Henrietta said.

"Leaping," Richard said. "I could be leaping."

Zeke looked down at Richard and then at Penelope. "I have no idea what's going on. Why would she stay in a cupboard?"

"The cupboard goes to another place," Henrietta said. "That's how we came through."

Zeke shrugged. "Whatever you say." He turned to Penelope. "I'll do what you want. I don't have time to figure all this out."

"Okay," she finally said. "We'll shove her through the cupboard."

Henrietta stood up. "I'll go turn the knobs."

"Why?" Penelope asked. "You just came through from somewhere. Can't she go there?"

Henrietta stopped, and then shook her head. "I don't want her there. It's sad enough already." Then she hurried from the room.

Zeke grabbed the witch's arm and pulled her toward the cupboard. Penelope tried to help. Anastasia was on the phone downstairs. Richard began humming.

When Henrietta reached the attic room, she looked around. It was very cold and strange with all the doors open. A tiny square of sunset poured through one, moonlight dribbled through another. Most were simply dark.

Different-flavored breezes played through Henrietta's hair. The room felt like it was breathing, like she was standing in a lung, with air moving in and out of the different cupboards. A cloud of dust was floating down from a small door near the top of the wall, and Henrietta could hear voices, singing, laughter, clinking glasses, knives scraping on plates. She went over to the wall, got down on her knees, and looked through the black cupboard. She picked up its door, shoved it on, and pushed the bed leg back against it. Then, starting on one side, she slammed every door she could reach.

When she got to the middle, she stopped. The door

with the compass locks was open, too. And there was something lumpy inside it, something charcoal gray. It was wheezing. She reached in and pulled out the small animal, and it sagged in her arms like a fat puppy. It had wings.

"Go ahead!" Zeke hollered from below. "Do whatever it is you're doing!" Henrietta tucked the animal in one arm, like she was carrying a baby, and shut the door. Then, with a quick flick, she spun the knobs.

"I think that's fine," Zeke called. "Doesn't look like there's a back." She turned and ran out of the room and down the stairs with her armload. She entered Grandfather's room as Zeke was fishing the witch's head into the cupboard. No one looked at her. Anastasia stood beside the body, gripping the witch's knife.

"What are you doing, Anastasia?" Penelope asked.

Anastasia smiled. "I'm just watching, in case she wakes up."

"You shouldn't keep that knife," Penelope said.

"Why not?"

"Because it's probably wicked or something."

Anastasia thought for a moment. "Maybe it was good first, and she stole it, and now it's good again."

"But you don't know that," Penelope said.

"You don't know it isn't," said Anastasia.

"Could you push on her legs?" Zeke asked. Penelope

bent down and grabbed the witch's leg. Then she shivered.

"She's freezing cold," she said.

"I know," Zeke answered. "I think she might die anyway. Unless she's always this cold. You push, too, Anastasia."

"But I'm making sure," Anastasia said.

Penelope glared at her. "Just put the knife down and push."

Anastasia did not want to, but she did. She set the knife on one of the bookshelves while she thought the others weren't looking, then stooped to push the cold body.

They had her through to the hips, so Zeke let go of her waist, moved behind the girls, and grabbed her ankles.

"This is the weirdest thing I've ever done," he said. "Weirdest I've ever seen." He braced himself and drove the witch through like a wheelbarrow. Both girls fell over, and Zeke landed on his knees. Then he moved his grip to the bottoms of her feet, and, puffing hard, pushed them in as well. When he was done, he stood, picked the knife up off the shelf, and threw it in the cupboard.

"Hey!" Anastasia said.

In the distance, they heard sirens.

"She's all in, Henrietta." Zeke turned to face her. "Is there anything we can do to keep her from just coming back through? What are you holding?"

Henrietta left and ran back up to the cupboards. She stood for a moment, facing the locks, trying to remember where they had been set before. She did not want to lose that place. She reset the compass locks and hurried back down the stairs to Grandfather's room.

Anastasia was frowning. Penelope was on the floor, running her hand through her father's hair.

"Well, she's gone," Zeke said. "Who knows where." The sirens were getting louder.

CHAPTER SEVENTEEN

The doctors at the small regional hospital were kept busy. Two ambulances brought in four patients for treatment, all from the same house. Francis H. Willis was treated for a stab wound in his side, severe concussion, and a partially collapsed lung. Dorothy S. Willis was treated for blood poisoning. Henry P. York was treated for burns to the jaw, slight skull fracture, and resulting concussion. Richard Hutchins was treated for a compound wrist fracture.

Penelope, Henrietta, and Anastasia Willis were all questioned individually, as was Ezekiel Johnson. They all told the same story, and the deputy who interviewed them retold it himself in the following weeks. It was always appreciated.

Frank Willis slipped at the top of the stairs while carrying a knife and took a visiting English cousin with him. He stabbed himself, but luckily he only broke the boy's arm. Everybody in the house ran to the commotion, including Dotty, who'd been frying bacon. She took the skillet with her, and when she saw the knife in old Frank's side, she fainted straight off. Henry, another cousin, tried to catch her but only took grease to the face and a doorknob to the back of the head for his trouble. Still, it was a good thing for Dotty that she did faint, or they might not have caught the blood poisoning.

Frank was the last to be released from the regional hospital. Dotty picked him up in the truck and drove him slowly through the field roads toward Henry, Kansas. They entered the city limits as quietly as the truck would allow and rolled past the burnt-out bus station and the old baseball field on their way to the tall house on the edge of town.

That night, wind brought in black clouds, and the rain came down sideways. Zeke came to dinner wet— Penelope had told him everything—and the family sat down around three loaves of meat. At the end of the meal, Dotty arched her eyebrows at Frank. He nodded and set down his fork.

"Well," he said, looking around the table. "This is the official meeting. We've all been through an adventure now, and here's where it ends. No more looking in cupboards. No more going through cupboards."

"But I never got to go through one," Anastasia said. "Not even once."

Frank smiled. "I know. And that's the way it's gonna stay." He looked at Penelope. "Penny, you get your own room now. Your mother and I are moving into Grandfather's room."

The kids all looked down at their plates, and Dotty blushed. "Frank," she said, "no one seems able to remember how, but during all the ruckus, the door shut again."

"Grandfather's door?" Frank asked. "Locked?"

Dotty smiled. "Yeah."

"Henrietta's got the key," Henry said. He sat up straight and looked at her.

"I did," Henrietta said. "But that was a long time ago. Has anyone seen it?"

Anastasia leaned over the table. "And she's keeping a baby rhino in the barn."

Henrietta sighed. Everyone was looking at her. "It's not a rhino. It looks a little like one, but it's way smaller."

"And it has wings," Anastasia said. "I followed her out there yesterday. She's feeding it cat food."

Zeke looked at Henrietta. "Is that what you were carrying?"

She nodded.

"Well," Frank said, "we're all here. Go get the rhino."

Henrietta came back into the dining room dripping with rain. Her arms were wrapped around something fat and gray with black, beady little eyes. She set it on the table and sat down.

It stood up on all fours, shook out gray feathered wings, and looked around the table. It was shaped almost exactly like a rhinoceros, only it was eighteen inches long and winged. It had one short, blunt horn, split and cracked at the end. Its belly hung almost to the ground, like a basset hound's.

"I haven't named him yet," Henrietta said. "And I can't get him to fly."

"I hope you don't think you're keeping it," Dotty said.

Frank was leaning forward, trying to look the thing in the eyes. He was smiling. "You aren't lookin' for me, are you?" he asked it.

"What is it?" Zeke asked.

Frank sat back up. "It's a raggant."

Dotty looked at him. "What?"

"A raggant. I've only ever seen two before. In some places, places I used to be, they're sent to find people. They can only be used once. When they've found someone, they stay till they die." He looked up at Henrietta. "Where did you get him?"

"He was in the cupboard with the compass locks. He'd been banging on the inside and broke his horn. He was almost dead and could barely move when I got him out."

Henry laughed and leaned forward. "You cracked my plaster, didn't you? You started the whole thing."

The raggant looked in Henry's eyes and snorted. He stepped toward him, lifted one of his front legs, and leaned, pointing, until his horn almost touched Henry's face.

"Ha!" Frank said. "It's Henry's!"

"What?" Henrietta said. "He's mine. I found him and fed him and took care of him!"

"We are not keeping it!" Dotty said.

Frank grinned. "Henry is."

The raggant turned and backed toward Henry, sat upright in front of him, tucked his wings back, and stared into space.

"Someone is lookin' for you, Henry," Frank said.

Henry felt nervousness bubble up inside him.

"Oh, don't worry," Frank added. "Raggants have never been used for any wickedness as far as I know."

"This isn't fair," Henrietta said. "I've never had a pet."

"You have Blake," Anastasia said, and she looked under the table, where the cat slept.

"Blake?" Henrietta said. "Blake's just another cat."

Zeke started laughing. Henrietta glared at him, but he didn't stop. She didn't say anything else.

"Frank," Dotty said. "We're not quite done."

"Right," Frank said. "I'll be plastering over all the

cupboards this weekend, and if I hear any late-night chipping, people are movin' into the barn. And if anyone finds the key to Grandfather's room, they'll immediately and without any sort of complaining turn it in to the Den Mother."

"That's me," Dotty said. In case anyone was confused.

When everyone had pushed back from empty plates, Dotty told the girls to clear the table. Zeke got up to help. Richard decided to watch and followed Anastasia into the kitchen. She made faces all the way. Frank stood slowly, put his hand on Henry's shoulder, and led him toward the front porch. The raggant walked proudly behind them.

The rain had stopped, but the world was still dark and wet. The wind was warm.

Frank eased himself into a rickety wicker chair and tucked a toothpick into his lip. Henry sat down on the top step and looked around for the raggant. It was perched on the porch rail with its nose toward the clouds and its wings spread in the breeze.

"Did it just fly, Uncle Frank?" Henry asked. "Did you see it?"

"Sure it did, but I didn't see anything. Raggants are proud, especially when they finish a job, so they don't like people to see them fly. Not sure why. Probably think it looks undignified."

The strange creature was really there. Henry could have reached out and touched it, but his mind still couldn't make sense of the animal. "Why would anyone be looking for me?" he asked.

"Well," Frank said, "because they lost you."

Henry stared at him. Frank pulled out his toothpick and examined the end. "I told you Phil and Urs aren't your parents, Henry."

"I thought I was adopted."

"Yeah," Frank said. "But, well, it wasn't a normal sort of adoption."

Henry waited for him to continue.

Frank looked at him. "Your grandfather always said he'd found you on the porch, but he was never Mr. Truth."

"I saw something in Grandfather's journal," Henry said, "something about me coming through the cupboards."

Frank leaned back in his chair.

"Do you think that could be true?" Henry asked. "Do you think I came from a different place?"

"In my experience," Frank said slowly, "when your grandfather found things, they were usually from the attic." Frank pointed his toothpick at the raggant. "Not many pets like that around here, for one."

Henry looked at the animal. Its blunted nose was still up, but it had shut its eyes.

Frank cleared his throat. "Dots and I wanted you, Henry. But Phil and Urs got the adoption. I've always felt guilty about it. Wished I could have changed things."

Henry looked at his uncle and at the clouds rolling above them. He looked at the raggant. The wind smelled like Badon Hill. "I'm not from here," he said.

"You and me both," Frank said. "But here's where we're from now."

The two of them sat silently and watched the world blow. And when the wind died, and the darkness grew thick, they listened to the raggant breathe, and to the laughter from the kitchen.

That night, Henry lay on his bed and felt his sore head and the newborn scar tissue along his jaw. He was looking at the ninety-nine doors on his wall, and thinking about the one downstairs.

He had already made sure the bed was against the black cupboard, and he felt better having the raggant around, anyway. It was snoring by his feet.

He rolled onto his side, facing away from the wall, and reached to turn off his lamp. When he did, he blinked. A beam of yellow light stood out through his room. He sat up and looked at the mailbox. There was another envelope inside. He looked at the door for a moment, then began hunting for the key. He found it underneath his socks.

When the door was open, he pulled out the letter, then crouched and stared at the yellow room for a while, hoping for a glimpse of the pants. They never came. Finally, he shut the little door and sat up. He looked over his wall. The raggant flared a wing out in its sleep and pawed at the blankets.

"I'm from one of these," he told the animal. "But you know that, don't you? You probably know which one."

Henry shifted to his knees and reached for the door to Badon Hill. Frank had said no more cupboards, but he knew his uncle would understand. He pulled the door open and sat back, just to smell the air and listen to the trees.

Something fluttered out of the darkness and landed on his bed.

Henry picked it up. It was another letter, folded and sealed with the green man. Two letters now. He shut the cupboard and looked at the two of them next to each other. They looked exactly like the first ones.

"I don't want these," he said out loud. "I'm done now."

He opened the long one first, and his eyes struggled with the writing.

Sir,
I take up this quill to anprass the magnappreciation of our order. Your hands bear prayse for they freed

the last Endorian blud. The old daughter of the
second sire regains her airth-strength. We kendle
her call.
Gratitation and fratri.
                    Darius,
                        First amung the Lastborn Magi,
                            Witch-Dog of Byzanthamum

Henry dropped the letter like it would stain his fingers and kicked it off his bed. It was still gibberish, but he understood it now. He had seen the Witch-Dogs work, or seen some spectral haunted dream of their working, and he wanted none of their gratitation. None of their anything.

He touched the green seal on the other letter, and when it popped, he unfolded the parchment. The same typed lines looked up at him.

Issuance from the Central Committee of
      Faeren for the Prevention of Mishap
(District R.R.K.)

Composed and Authorized by Committee
      Chair under Executive Guidelines
(B.F. X.vii)

Delivered via the Island Hill of Badon
Chapter
(District A.P.)

To Whom We Have Concerned:
It is the finding of the committee
that Whimpering Child (hereafter: WC)
has aided, abetted, and enabled the
unearthing and potential
reestablishment of old evil and is a
danger to the faeren people, himself,
and the tapestry of reality. WC shall
henceforth be identified as Enemy,
Hazard, and Human Mishap to all faeren
in all districts, all worlds, and all
ways.

Identification has been distributed
and status change documented. Where
and when WC is encountered, the
committee has authorized, yea,
demanded, that he be hampered,
hindered, detained, damaged, or
destroyed. Such treatment, performed
by any faeren of any district, way, or
world, shall be deemed just, necessary,
merciful, and inevitable.

Ralph Radulf
Chair CCFPM
    (District R.R.K.)
C and A by CC under EG
    (per B.F. X.vii)
Delivered via Island Hill
    of Badon Chapter
    (District A.P.)

Henry flopped back onto his bed and stared at the poster on his ceiling. Then he kicked his wall. He hadn't asked for this. He hadn't wanted to free a witch. He'd actually had very little to do with it. Well, he had chipped all the plaster off his wall and uncovered the cupboards. There was that. But that hadn't even been his fault. He propped himself up.

"That was you," he said to the raggant, and poked it with his toe. "You had to start thumping in there."

The raggant's skin quaked, like a horse shaking off a fly, and it sat up. Its black eyes stared at Henry, and then it yawned and walked onto Henry's legs. Henry flopped back again, and the raggant crawled onto his chest and curled up into a wheezing ball.

Henry smiled. "Your fault," he said again. "I did nothing. I'm just scenery."

* * *

Downstairs, Dotty opened her eyes. "Frank?"

Frank grunted.

She sat up and reached for her bathrobe. "Henry York, you'd better not be doing what I think you're doing."

Frank's hand pulled her back down.

"He'll be fine," he said.

EPILOGUE

The cat was large, used to feeding on the rubbish and scrapings thrown out the kitchen window and occasionally on the also overfed and lazy rats. He was a tom, black, with a white face and tail. He had no name that he knew of, but someone was calling for him. That someone wanted him. Needed him.

He did not usually venture up into the room where the old man sat, the room with the gaping doors and the moon windows. The doors made his spine tingle and his pads cold. But this time he leapt up the stairs with his belly swinging below him. He passed the cold body of a young wizard sprawled at the top. And then two others, and between them, the body of a dog.

Once he was in the throne room, the calling thrilled him, filling his mind and all his senses. And there, standing inside one of the thickly curtained doorways and facing a young man, an orderly still on his feet, was a woman. To the cat's mind, she was both old and young, weak and strong. All-seeing but in need of his wisdom, his sight. He leapt into the woman's arms, and she was inside him, his mind was with hers, and then, in a moment, his was gone.

"What is your name?" the woman asked the man.

The young man did not look away from her. "Monmouth," he said. "What is yours?"

The woman laughed, filling the stone hall with her echoes. "You are not even an apprenticed wizard, and you ask me this? I have fed myself on the lives of your masters who lie cold behind you, and you stand to request my name?" She stepped toward him.

"I do," he said, and did not so much as shift his feet.

She stepped even closer, stroking the heavy cat's head. "Then wake your doddering master Carnassus, and tell him this, if your mouth will hold the words: Nimiane, dread Queen of Endor, last in Niac's line, whose voice destroyed the magic of FitzFaeren, boiled up the sea to shatter the strength of Amram, and laid Merlinis to rest beneath the wood, once bound by Mordecai, Amram's son, has shaken off her chains as her fathers shook off the blood of Adam, and comes to see if an old man remembers vows he made when he was young.

"New prey waits on the Witch-Dogs."

GRATITUDE

Mark B. for imagining. Neighbor Cousins for listening. Heather for being. Jim T. for hacking, shaping, sanding, and, eventually, liking.

The world-hopping adventure continues!

Dandelion Fire

✦ BOOK II ✦
of The 100 Cupboards

*Available in February 2009
from Random House Books for Young Readers.*

CHAPTER ONE

Kansas is not easily impressed. It has seen houses fly and cattle soar. When funnel clouds walk through the wheat, big hail falls behind. As the biggest stones melt, turtles and mice and fish and even men can be seen frozen inside. And Kansas is not surprised.

Henry York had seen things in Kansas, things he didn't think belonged in this world. Things that didn't. Kansas hadn't flinched.

The soles of Henry's shoes were twenty feet off the ground. He had managed to slide open the heavy door in the barn loft, and after brushing the rust and flakes of red paint off his hands, he'd seated himself on the dust-covered planks and looked out over the ripening fields. Henry's feet dangled, but Kansas sprawled.

Henry had changed in the short weeks since he'd stepped off the bus from Boston, been smothered by Aunt Dotty and taken to the old farmhouse, to the attic—to a new existence. He looked different, too, and it wasn't just the cut across the backs of his fingers. That was scarring worse than it needed to only because he couldn't stop himself from picking at it. The burns on his jaw were a lot more noticeable and had begun scarring as well. He didn't like touching them. But he had to. Especially the one below his ear. It was turning into a divot as wide as his fingertip.

What had changed most about Henry York was inside his head. Things he had always known no longer seemed true. A world that had always felt like a slow and stable and even boring machine had suddenly come to life. And it was far from tame. He'd uncovered a wall of doors in his attic room, and now he didn't know who he was. He didn't know who his real parents were or whether he was even in the right world. He didn't really know anything. Strangely, that was more comfortable than thinking that he did.

One month before, fresh off the bus from Boston, he would have been nervous sitting where he was, slowly bouncing his heels on the wall of the barn. One month before, he wouldn't have believed that he could hit a baseball. Something wheezed beside him, and Henry turned. One month before, the world was still normal, and creatures like this one didn't exist.

The raggant sniffed loudly and settled onto his haunches. His wings were tucked back against his rough charcoal skin and his blunt horn was, as always, lifted in the air.

Henry smiled. He always did when he looked at the animal. It was so proud and so very unaware of how it looked. At least Henry thought it had to be. Shaped like a small basset hound but wearing wings and a rhino's face and skin, it was far from beautiful, but that didn't stop it from being as proud and stubborn as a peacock. Like an otherworldly bloodhound, it had found Henry, cracking the plaster in the attic wall from inside a cupboard. The raggant had started everything. Whoever it was that had sent the raggant had started everything. Henry couldn't even imagine who that might be.

"Do you know how strange you look?" Henry asked, and he reached over and grabbed the loose skin on the creature's neck. It felt like sand-based dough, and as he squeezed, the raggant closed its black eyes and a low moan sputtered in its chest.

"I want to see you fly," Henry said. "You know I will." He glanced down at the ground and then back at the raggant. He could push it. Then it would have to fly. But it just might be proud enough not to, proud enough to tuck its wings tight and bounce in the tall grass. "Sometime," Henry said.

The afternoon sun was falling, and Henry knew it wouldn't be long before the barn's shadow stretched across acres. Worse, it wouldn't be long before the fields and the barn and all of Kansas became part of his past. His parents had been back from their ill-fated bicycle trip for a while, and he still hadn't heard from them. That wasn't too unusual. When they were just getting back from their photographed adventures, he rarely ever heard from them. The fact that they'd actually managed to get kidnapped this time would make their return crazier, would keep him safely off their minds for that much longer. But it couldn't last. If they'd had any say in the matter, he never would have been sent to stay with his cousins at all. Now that they'd returned, they wouldn't leave him in Kansas for school or even through the summer. He'd be back in Boston, on some new vitamin diet and meeting a new nanny, and then back to boarding school. Maybe a new one. His third.

Parents. He still thought of them that way. Would they ever have told him that Grandfather had found him in the attic? Not likely. Henry didn't care that he'd been adopted. But it was hard not to care that his parents had never really been parents—not like Uncle Frank and Aunt Dotty were to his cousins. Henry had always known exactly where he was on his parents' list of priorities.

Yesterday, he'd seen his parents on television. He'd been stirring his cereal and listening to his youngest cousin, Anastasia, complain about Richard when Uncle Frank called him. He'd hurried, and when he stepped into the room, Frank pointed. There, on a stiff couch in a television studio somewhere, sat Phillip and Ursula, smiling and nodding. They each had hands crossed on their knees. Ursula kept glancing at the camera. She looked like Henry's aunt Dotty, but with all her edges hardened. The two of them talked about their amazing endurance, the difficulty of bicycling through the Andes, how they had never given up hope of finishing their trek even after being abducted in Colombia, the size of their book deal, and their discussions with film agents.

In a general way, Henry remembered all they had said. But there were two things that sat in the front of his mind, every syllable in concrete.

"Are you closer now?" the woman had asked them. "After going through all of this together?"

Ursula had leaned forward. Phillip had leaned back. "You know," Ursula had said. "We've both changed a great deal during this whole process. We really need to get to know each other again. But first we need to get to know ourselves."

Phillip had nodded.

Henry was pretty sure he knew what that meant.

And then the woman had asked about him.

"Now you all have a son? Is that right?"

"That's right," Phillip had said.

Ursula had smiled. "Our little Henry."

"That must have been quite the reunion. What went through your minds when you saw him again?"

"Oh, it was wonderful," Ursula had said. "Elation. Pure maternal elation."

"Thrilling," Phillip had said.

It had been strange, watching his parents lie. Uncle Frank had slapped his shoulder afterward and Aunt Dotty had squeezed him. Anastasia had opened her mouth, but Penelope, the oldest, always the most concerned, had pinched her before she could say anything. Henrietta had tucked back her curls and stared at him.

The two of them had opened the doors together, had knelt in the attic and stared into strange worlds, and still she always tested him, curious if he'd be weak. Henry knew she was waiting to see if he'd be sad. He hadn't been. Not then. Richard, always out of place, had stepped quickly out of the room.

"What am I going to do?" Henry asked the raggant. "I won't get to stay here, and you can't come with me even if you try. You'd get sold to a zoo. Or a circus."

A hot breeze crawled through the fields, rolling the surface like thick liquid. The raggant didn't open its eyes, but its nostrils flared.

"Richard is worse," Henry said. The scrawny boy who'd followed him back through the cupboards into Kansas weighed on his mind a lot. "Unless he lives here forever, he'll have to go back through the cupboards. Maybe not home, but somewhere else. Unless Anastasia kills him first."

Below Henry, from the other side of the barn, came the sound of an old door rattling open.

"Henry of York!" Uncle Frank yelled.

Henry turned. "Yeah?" Footsteps crossed the plank floor below him. They stopped. Old ladder rungs sighed.

Five feet from where Henry and the raggant sat, Uncle Frank's head emerged. Henry smiled at him, but Uncle Frank didn't smile back. He was looking past his nephew, out the open doorway and into the fields. When he'd pulled his thin body up, he scratched the raggant's chin and then sat down beside Henry. His eyes wandered across the sky and then down through the wheat sea.

"Careful, Henry," he said. "Place like this can get in your bones. Even if you don't care for it, leaving can hurt more than it needs to."

Henry looked into his uncle's face, lean and leathery, with his eyes hooded toward the horizon like a sailor looking for land he knows he'll never find. His face didn't really explain his words. It never did. His uncle had tumbled into Kansas as a teenager, another victim of the cupboards. Henry wondered how long it would be before he looked like Frank, until he looked like something borrowed and never returned, out of place but settled in and dusty. At least Uncle Frank had memories. He knew what he'd lost, though he didn't talk about it. Henry didn't even have that.

Frank popped his knuckles and leaned back. "You can smell when the fields go green. And gold. Sound different, too. Green field rustles. Gold rattles."

"When's the harvest?" Henry asked.

"Soon," Frank said. "When the gold aims for white. You'll see the combines roll even if you don't see 'em finish."

Henry watched the wind work. "I have to leave, don't I?"

"Yep."

"I wish I didn't."

"Well," Frank said. "If wishes were horses."

Henry looked at him. "Then what?" he asked.

"Then I'd have a horse."

Henry almost smiled. He'd expected something like that. Beside him, the raggant snored. Still sitting up, its jaw hung open; its head sagged, nose no longer in the air. Henry eased it onto its side. "I wish I knew how long I have," Henry said. "I don't even like being in the house. Every time the phone rings, I think someone's on their way to pick me up."

"July third," Frank said. "Two weeks. Got a letter today."

"What?" Henry asked. "Why the third? Who sent the letter?"

Frank straightened his leg and dug his hand into the pocket of his jeans. He dropped an envelope, warm and wrinkled, onto Henry's lap. "Came up here to tell you. It's from a lawyer. Phil and Urs are parting ways. They've got some sort of custody arranging to handle next week. They'll figure out which one gets you, and then you'll leave."

Henry opened the letter and stared at it. It was addressed to his aunt and uncle, and there wasn't anything more to it than Uncle Frank had already told him.

"Two weeks," Henry said. "I'll miss the fireworks."

"Could be shorter," Frank said. "Moon goes halfway round the world in two weeks."

The two of them sat, and the raggant snored. After a while, Frank stood and stretched.

"Anastasia will call for you when supper's set," he said, and stepped toward the ladder.

Henry nodded. He didn't watch his uncle leave.

When Anastasia's voice reached him, Henry's legs still hung out the doorway, but he was on his back. He sat up and looked at the letter in his hand. He folded it up and slid it into the envelope.

"Henry!" Anastasia yelled again.

"Coming!" he said, and then flicked the envelope out onto the wind. He watched it spin as it dropped to the swaying tall grass beside the barn. "Go where you want," he said, and he stood up.

He left the raggant sleeping and climbed down the ladder. Anastasia had already gone back inside.

The table was crowded, but only Anastasia seemed to want to talk. Henry and Richard sat on one side, facing Henry's three cousins. Richard was wearing a tight yellow sweatshirt with a cantering pony on the front, forcibly borrowed from Anastasia. He was picking at the blue cast on his wrist. Uncle Frank sat with eyes unfocused and fork frozen in his hand while Aunt Dotty spread a smile, scooped buttered noodles, and passed plates. Henry looked at Penelope. She pushed her long black hair out of her face and smiled at him with lips clamped tight. Beside her sat Henrietta, curls loose and chin on her hand. She was staring at Henry again, but when their eyes met, she looked down to where her plate would be as soon as her mother gave it back. Beside her, Anastasia, shortest in her chair, chattered cheerfully.

"When Henry leaves, we'll have to keep the raggant, won't we? You should have named him a long time ago, Henry. I'll write you a letter and tell you what we name him. Do you want me to do that?"

Henry looked at her and shrugged. She looked at Richard.

"What are we going to do with Richard?" Anastasia asked. "He can't live here forever, wearing my clothes."

"Don't be rude," Penelope said.

Anastasia looked shocked. "I'm not being. Mom?"

Dotty nodded. "Be polite." Passing the last plate, she sat back in her chair and puffed stray, frizzing hairs off her forehead.

"I'm not being rude," Anastasia said. "I'm just being honest. We should send him back through the cupboards."

"Anastasia!" Dotty said.

Richard looked up, his thin, blotchy face even blotchier above the yellow shirt. "If I am going to be discussed," he said with eyebrows raised, "I would rather not be present."

"No," Dotty said quickly.

"I want my clothes back," Anastasia muttered.

"Frank?" Dotty asked. "Could you be here, please? In this world, with us. Just for now."

Frank took a deep breath, coming awake. "We couldn't send him back if we wanted. Not without the big cupboard in Grandfather's room, and that bedroom door is magicked right back to unbudgeable, isn't it? I'm not trying the chain saw again, and the attic cupboards are too small even if we folded him in thirds."

"I can't believe we're talking about this," Dotty said. "Frank Willis, you promised to plaster over those cupboards, and no one was to even think about traveling through them. Do you *want* something to happen?"

For a moment, Frank sat perfectly still, his jaw no longer chewing, his hand in the air above his plate. Then he spoke. "Doesn't matter. Don't have Grandfather's key." And he spun himself another forkful of noodles.

Henry was thinking the same thing. He had a wall of doors in his attic bedroom, none of them leading to Boston, one of them leading back to his birth-world and the world the raggant had come from. But it didn't matter. The cupboards up in his attic were like little windows, linking other places to this one, but they were no good to him unless they channeled through the cupboard in Grandfather's room, the one big enough for him to crawl through. He had Grandfather's journal with the combinations to connect each of his little doors to the bigger cupboard, but without Grandfather's key, there was no point.

"Henrietta's got the key," Anastasia said. "I've told you a hundred times, but you won't listen."

Henrietta banged her fork down onto the table and rolled her eyes. "I don't have anything."

"It's not in any of her normal hiding places," Anastasia continued. "But I'll find it."

Henry stood up. "Do you mind if I go up to my room?" he asked his aunt. "I'm not real hungry."

Dotty looked in his face, her eyebrows lifted. "What are you going to do?"

Henry halfway smiled. "Nothing," he said. "I don't have Grandfather's key."

When he reached the big second-story landing, Henry stopped. Anastasia's voice was mixing with Henrietta's, but he pushed the noise out of his head. He was looking at Grandfather's knobless door. Chopped and chewed and even cursed, it was still shut tight, impossible to re-open without the key. Any hope of finding where he'd come from was behind that door.

Henry walked around the railing and stood directly in front of the mutilated wood panels. With his toe, he prodded the tangled mess of carpet where Frank had dipped the chain saw. He'd lain right there with the hands of Nimiane of Endor around his neck. Her blood had burned his face like acid. His throat constricted at the memory, and his stomach queezed. Shivering, he hurried back around the landing to the steep attic stairs.

There were worse things than going back to Boston.

In the long, coved attic, Richard's sleeping bag and a small stack of borrowed clothes were piled against the wall beside Henry's closet room. Richard had wanted to sleep on the floor at the end of Henry's bed, but this arrangement was as close to room-sharing as Henry was willing to go.

Once inside his room, Henry went through what had become his entrance ritual. He turned on his light and stood back to examine the wall of cupboard doors. Ninety-nine doors of all shapes and sizes looked back at him. His eyes were first drawn to the center, where the door with the two compass knobs ruled the wall. It wasn't the most ornate of the doors, but, with the right combination, it could channel any of the others through the larger cupboard downstairs in Grandfather's room. And it had been the raggant's entrance into Kansas.

After letting his eyes run over the deep grains and bright inlay, flaking varnish and rusted hinges, the different colors, textures, and shapes, Henry next stepped to his bed. He pulled it away from the wall, where it hid half of the bottom two rows. He held his breath, forced himself to crouch at the foot, and looked directly at the black door on the bottom row with the gold knob in the center. Door number 8. The door to Endor.

Henry finger-checked the four screws Uncle Frank had used to seal it, stood up quickly, and pushed his bed leg back against it. Then he breathed. He knew that Nimiane wasn't behind that door anymore. She was behind whichever door his cousins had randomly selected while he and the witch had been unconscious. He'd heard the story, the description of the bat hitting her head, her cold skin. Anastasia still insisted that they should have stabbed her in the neck. But they hadn't. Afraid she would wake up, they'd fished her through the big cupboard and into some unlucky world. She wasn't in Endor anymore, but Henry still found the screws re-assuring.

When Henry was breathing again, he found door number 56, the door to the place called Badon Hill, and opened it. He sat on his bed and waited for the air from that other place to drift in. It always did, and when the smell of moss and rain and a wind that had toppled breakers and poured through trees surrounded him, then Henry considered himself to actually *be* in his room.

Henry lay back on his bed and sighed. The doors frightened him, but they drew him as well. Behind one was the world where he'd been born, where he had siblings. At least six older brothers, if he believed what the old wizard had said in the cold throne room when he'd first gone through the cupboards. He looked up the wall at door number 12. Richard had crawled into that world behind him, and the wizard had known who Henry was. He would be able to tell Henry where he was really from. But he'd been horrible. Henry shifted his thoughts away from the memory and back to the doors in front of him. There was no reason to think that he'd come from a nice place, that the bent old man eating grubs on his dark throne had told the truth, or that his family was alive, and if they were, that they even wanted him. Wanted babies weren't usually shoved into cupboards.

But there was still the raggant. Raggants were for finding things. Someone had wanted to find him.

Henry took a deep breath and puffed out his cheeks.

Why had Uncle Frank stopped trying to get back? Was he afraid, too? But Frank had Dotty and his daughters. No one was going to put him on a bus back to Boston in two weeks.

"Two weeks," Henry said out loud. He looked over to the corner of his room, where one week ago, Frank had left a small roll of chicken wire and a five-gallon bucket of plaster. The wire was to cover the cupboards and strengthen the plaster. Frank hadn't touched it since he'd put it there. He'd mixed the plaster, but then left it. Now the bucket was as solid as a boulder.

"I could come back when I'm eighteen," Henry said. But he didn't think Frank could put Dotty off that long. A couple years, maybe, but not more than five.

Someone was coming up the attic stairs. Henry sat up on his bed and quietly shut the open cupboard.

His bedroom doors swung open, and Henrietta stepped into his room. She had the raggant tucked under one arm. It dropped quickly to the floor and jumped onto Henry's bed.

Henrietta sniffed the air, and her eyes drifted to the cupboard to Badon Hill. They hadn't talked in a while, and for a moment, they were both silent.

"Henrietta," Henry said. "I need Grandfather's key."

She met Henry's eyes and stared right through.

"There's no point in lying to me," Henry continued. "Things got really crazy at the end, but I know I didn't keep it, and you were the only other one who could have."

Henrietta crossed her arms and looked at the wall of

doors. Henry rambled on. "I'd be happy to stay here, but I can't. Two weeks, Henrietta, and then I go back to Boston and then back to school, and over the summers they'll store me somewhere, and I won't be able to come back until I'm old enough to move out or go to college." Henry took a breath. "I can't be here when they come for me. I have to go through the cupboards. And you have the key, Henrietta. You have to give it to me."

Henrietta sat down on the bed beside him.

"I know," she said. "I buried it behind the barn."

Have you read N. D. Wilson's breathtaking debut?

LEEPIKE RIDGE

★ "This is a ripping good adventure yarn."
—*The Bulletin of the Center for Children's Books*, Starred

"While *Leepike Ridge* is primarily an adventure story involving murder, treachery, and betrayal, Wilson's rich imagination and his quirky characters are a true delight.... There are enough twists and turns in the plot to keep both seasoned and reluctant readers turning the pages." —*School Library Journal*

"Wilson sets the scene vividly, from Tom's home to the labyrinth of tunnels and caverns under the mountain, and the central characters' emotional lives develop both naturally and affectingly.... [Readers] will appreciate both the fast-paced adventure and Tom's determination to make the impossible journey back home." —*The Horn Book Magazine*

"Wilson's debut is a literate, sometimes humorous page-turner in the classic tradition. Well-read adventure lovers are in for a treat looking for echoes of *The Odyssey* and *Tom Sawyer*." —*Kirkus Reviews*

"Tom's adventures have several literary ancestors, including Tom and Huck in the cave, and the inventive *Swiss Family Robinson*, but this is solidly set in the present, standing on its own with well-crafted suspense and fascinating survival detail.... [Readers will] relish the physicality of the journey: underwater swims, tight passages, and rock climbing." —*Booklist*